I0672875

Body
in the
Bay

A Mark Daniels Mystery

Body
in the
Bay

A Mark Daniels Mystery

Book Three

Justin Maxwell

ABSOLUTELY AMA⚡ING eBOOKS

ABSOLUTELY AMAZING eBOOKS

Published by Whiz Bang LLC, 926 Truman Avenue, Key West, Florida 33040, USA.

Body in the Bay copyright © 2018 by Wayne Kadar. Electronic compilation/ paperback edition copyright © 2018 by Whiz Bang LLC. Cover Photograph of Florida Bay by Karen Kadar.

All rights reserved. No part of this book may be reproduced, scanned, or transmitted in any form or by any means, electronic or mechanical, including photocopying, recording, or any information storage and retrieval system, without permission in writing from the publisher. Please do not participate in or encourage piracy of copyrighted materials in violation of the author's rights. Purchase only authorized ebook editions.

This is a work of fiction. Names, characters, places, and incidents either are the product of the author's imagination or are used fictitiously, and any resemblance to actual persons, living or dead, businesses, companies, events, or locales is entirely coincidental. While the author has made every effort to provide accurate information at the time of publication, neither the publisher nor the author assumes any responsibility for errors, or for changes that occur after publication. Further, the publisher does not have any control over and does not assume any responsibility for author or third-party websites or their contents. How the ebook displays on a given reader is beyond the publisher's control.

For information contact:
Publisher@AbsolutelyAmazingEbooks.com

ISBN-13: 978-1949504231 (Absolutely Amazing Ebooks)
ISBN-10: 1949504239

This book is dedicated to the resilient residents of the Florida Keys who took all Hurricane Irma had to throw at them and came out punching back.

"Like the palm trees that are so plentiful on the islands, the Keys residents bent but they didn't break."

Body
in the
Bay

A Mark Daniels Mystery

Chapter One

Sherry backed the trailer down the ramp, Mark released the bowline and the 15-foot hard bottom inflatable boat floated free. He lowered the outboard into the water and turned the key. The four-stroke engine started instantly and purred like a kitten. He let the Mercury warm up, then lowered the throttle handle and slowly backed away. He gave Sherry a thumbs-up and she pulled the trailer up the ramp and headed back to the condo and Mark turned towards open water.

Normally he would slam the throttle down to feel the acceleration of the horsepower, but after last year when he got mixed up with murderous modern-day pirates chasing Spanish treasure, Mark vowed this winter's four month stay in the Florida Keys would be relaxing and stress-free. He eased the throttle to a leisurely pace to enjoy the sun, blue sky and calm water of Florida Bay.

Mark relaxed and watched a circling pelican dive into the water and come up with a fish. Seagulls screamed while they chased the pelican, hoping he would drop his lunch.

About a mile into the trip to the condo dock, Mark noticed a fish scurrying along the bottom. He slowed to watch the three-foot nurse shark swimming along the sandy bottom. He smiled thinking of the first time he saw a nurse shark. He was sure it was going to leap out the water and take a bite out of the boat like in the movie *Jaws*.

In the clear water of Florida Bay there were all kinds of creatures to entertain him; the lobster that lived in the crevices of the coral, bonefish that inhabited the mudflats to feed on creatures traveling on the incoming tide, and the huge gentle manatee that often visited the condo dock.

As Mark slowly cruised, he noticed a dark shadow in the water ahead. He slowed to see a good size Spotted Eagle Ray skimming across the sandy bottom. "That is the biggest ray I've seen," Mark said as he watched the graceful creature "flying" along the bottom. "I bet it's more than three feet across!" He watched the ray until it swam out of view.

Mark was enjoying the slower pace and taking time to smell the roses, or in this case, watch nature, as he slowly puttered along. Off in the distance Mark saw what appeared to be the rounded back of a sea turtle floating at the surface. He wondered what kind it was. "From here it looks like a loggerhead or maybe a leatherback," Mark thought, trying to remember what he learned from their tour at the Turtle Hospital in Marathon. "My guess is a loggerhead."

He stopped the engine and let the boat slowly drift forward and was amazed the turtle didn't submerge and swim away. As he got closer he realized it wasn't a turtle. It was a dead body.

A corpse was floating face down, its arms out to the sides, its head drooping and its legs hanging down. The arched back at the surface gave it the appearance of the shell of a turtle.

The bow wave of the boat caused the body to drift. Knowing he had to keep the body from floating away or sinking before the authorities arrived, Mark instinctively reached out for its hand.

As Mark grasped the pale white, wrinkled hand and began to pull, the skin of the hand peeled away like a glove, leaving Mark holding a mushy handful of putrid flesh. He shook his hand in disgust releasing the slimy material, it fell into his lap. He quickly stood up and brushed the rotten flesh into the water.

To keep the rotting corpse from slipping away, Mark slipped a dock line around the torso. He carefully pulled the figure towards the boat, the body rolled on its side revealing a face bleached white and bloated from saltwater. Sea life had been feeding on it. The soft tissue of the lips and nose were gone and there were two empty sockets where the eyes had been devoured by shrimp, crabs and other sea creatures.

Mark held the rope tight against the boat as he removed his cell phone from his pocket. One handed, he dialed 911 and lifted the phone to his ear. He heard the operator answer but the stench of putrefied flesh on his hand was unbearable. He began gagging, dropped the phone to the deck and retched over the side.

Mark wiped his mouth with his forearm and picked up the phone, turning on the speaker function. The emergency operator was still on the line asking, "Hello? Hello? 911. What's your emergency? Is there anyone there? What is your emergency?"

Trying to repress his gag reflex Mark said, "I ... I found ... ah ... a body in the bay!" He gave his coordinates for the Coast Guard to come take the corpse off his hands ... literally.

As he waited, Mark wanted to dip his hand in the water to rid it of the foul odor and any residue of rotting flesh, but he was tiring and had to use both hands on the line to hold the body. Sea gulls circled above screeching and small fish were in a feeding frenzy as they picked at the putrid flesh of the hand lying six feet below on the sandy bottom.

He could hear a siren in the distance then saw the flashing blue lights and orange hull of a Coast Guard boat racing towards him.

The vessel slowed as it approached Mark's boat. Two Coasties in flotation suits entered the water and carefully took the body from Mark and floated it onto a backboard.

Once it was secured, the body was lifted aboard the rescue boat.

In his natural journalistic inquisitiveness, Mark looked at the body as it was raised up onto the Coast Guard boat. He noticed both the right foot and right hand were missing. Mark thought to himself, "Don't blame those on me, I only peeled the left hand."

A Coast Guardsman, with a rag tied around his head covering his nose, gagged as he questioned Mark. He answered the questions and provided the Coast Guard his personal information while another Coast Guardsman handed him a sliver of soap. Mark dipped his hands in the water working up a lather hoping to get rid of the disgusting odor. Instead it left his hands smelling like a decomposing corpse in an Irish spring.

The Coast Guard vessel cast off its lines from Mark's boat and slowly powered away. Mark started his engine, slammed the throttle down full and sped towards the condo.

As he powered to the dock he said to himself, "After a career of chasing death as a reporter and last year's murders involving Spanish treasure, I was going to relax this winter, but here I am with a dead body on my hands. Actually on my hands."

Racing across the water Mark slipped into journalist mode. "I wonder how long the corpse has been in the water? I wonder if the body is from a boating accident, possibly a person blown offshore during Hurricane Irma, or maybe someone trying to hide the evidence of a murder."

Mark wouldn't relax until he knew who the rotting corpse was and how he died. He said aloud, "So much for a calm relaxing winter in the Keys."

Chapter Two

That evening at the first Condominium Snowbird Sunset Celebration Mark was besieged with questions. They weren't the questions usually asked when greeting friends not seen in months. The questions weren't; "How have you been? Did you have a good summer? How was the fishing up north?" Rather they were questions like; "Who was the dead guy? How long was he in the water? Is he a local? Do you think he was an illegal trying to sneak into the country? Think maybe he is a victim of the hurricane?"

Mark just responded that he didn't know anything about the guy other than he was quite dead.

After finding the body in the bay, Mark tied up at the condo dock, quickly sprayed the boat down then ran to the condo and poured bleach on his hands trying to get rid of the putrid odor. He took a long shower, scrubbing himself twice and yet as he stood at the sunset celebration he could still smell the odor of rotting flesh. Since no one backed away or pinched their nose as they talked with him, Mark decided the odor was only in his mind.

That night as Sherry slept, Mark laid awake staring at the ceiling. Throughout his career as a reporter for the Detroit Free Press specializing in murder cases, he had seen many dead bodies; people who had been shot in the back of the head with half of their face missing, victims pulled out of the Detroit River, people beaten to death, and he still vividly remembered the woman who was pushed beneath a moving train. But he had never touched the bodies. He never grabbed one only to have the flesh peel off like a slimy glove.

As he remembered discovering the body, the odor of rotting flesh crept back into his mind.

He asked himself the questions the Coast Guard and his neighbors asked earlier. "Who was he? Why was he in the bay? "Hell, I guess I don't even know if it was a man. The body was so bloated and decayed it might have been a woman."

With the ceiling fan slowly spinning above him, Mark's mind slipped into investigative reporter mode. He wondered how they would be able to determine who the victim was. "Surely no one can recognize the corpse's face, and they won't be able to get finger prints; the right hand is missing and the fingertips of the left hand are working through the digestive track of a bunch of fish."

"Maybe DNA?" he thought. "They can identify the victim through DNA. That is if submersion in saltwater hasn't destroyed it. But, they can identify a victim by using the DNA from bone marrow so they should be able to identify the body. The salt water shouldn't have destroyed the bone marrow," Mark theorized.

"Wait a minute," he corrected himself. "They should be able to obtain DNA from the corpse but they still may not be able to identify the victim. That will depend on whether his or her DNA had been collected and cataloged when the victim was alive."

With the odor of the rotting hand creeping into his mind Mark mumbled, "I've got to get some sleep." He turned on his side and buried his head in the pillow hoping it would shut off his brain and his imaginary sense of smell.

~ ~ ~

Despite being up late thinking about the body in the bay, Mark awoke early. It was his normal routine, get up between 6:00 and 6:30, start a pot of coffee, and sit on the balcony of their condominium. With his laptop on his lap,

Mark sat and worked on his second novel.

Mark sipped his coffee and smelled the unmistakable scent of bacon frying from a condo a couple of doors down. He closed his eyes and took a deep breath to titillate his olfactory senses with the meaty fragrance he had not smelled since Sherry put them on a healthy eating regiment. He enjoyed the fragrance until his mind morphed from the delectable aroma to the pungent odor of rotting flesh. Mark quickly opened his eyes bringing himself back to reality hoping to rid his mind of the disgustingly foul smell. It didn't work.

He opened email to read the latest joke his sister sent. "I swear she is the only person who still forwards jokes on email."

The diversionary tactic worked, the odor faded. Rotting flesh, no longer polluted his brain. Mark checked the local online newspaper, *The Island Times*, hoping to find an article about the body he found in the bay. Although, he didn't anticipate much until later in the day when a reporter had an opportunity to investigate and write an article.

But there was a headline, "Body discovered in Bay." It was just a brief article saying a body was found by a boater and the sheriff's department was investigating. Pretty much what he expected. An initial article with more to follow.

Mark heard Sherry stirring upstairs. As per their normal morning routine, he got up to mix her morning elixir and had it waiting on the table between their chairs when she appeared.

"Good morning beautiful," Mark said to his wife.

"Did you find anything about the body online?" she asked, knowing Mark's inquisitive mind would be seeking information about the corpse.

"Just a quick article saying a body was found by a boater."

"Hey, you got your name in the newspaper, you're the

boater," she said with a giggle.

He smiled at his wife and took a sip of his coffee. He opened the computer but before it could boot up there was a knock on their door. Expecting a neighbor inviting Sherry out for a walk or someone wanting to plan a lady's lunch, Mark was surprised to find a young woman he didn't know standing at the door.

"Hello, may I help you?" he asked.

"Ah, hello ... Ah, Mr. Daniels, I'm Rebecca Cory a reporter with *The Island Times*," she stammered. "Ah, do you have a few minutes to talk to me?

Mark was cautions about inviting strangers into his house, a trait he developed after years of dealing with the criminal element he worked with as a reporter. The woman at the door looked to be in her mid to late twenties, she held a notebook in one hand and nervously twirled a pen between her fingers in the other. She wore a lanyard around her neck with a laminated identification card printed with her name, photograph and the beach and palm tree logo of *The Island Times*.

Mark figured she was okay and invited her in.

Sherry walked in from the balcony and offered the young woman a drink, "Coffee, iced tea? Water?"

"Thank you I would like an iced tea, please," she responded, obviously nervous. Mark could tell she was not comfortable, he had seen it hundreds of times with young reporters. He asked, "How can I help you Ms. Cory?

"Please Mr. Daniels call me Becca. Or my brothers call me R.C." she said.

"Okay, Becca but this is Sherry and I'm Mark."

"Alright," she said. "Ah, if you don't mind I would like to... ah... interview you about the body you found yesterday."

Becca was obviously uncomfortable. Mark figured she must be new on the job. To try to set her at ease, he asked,

"How long have you been working for *The Island Times*?"

"I've been there about a year and a half and before that I worked for the *Sentinel Tribune* in Bowling Green, and in college I interned at the *Dayton Daily News*."

"Sounds like you have a lot of experience." Mark encouraged her. "Go ahead, shoot some questions at me."

Becca gave a slight smile, took a deep breath and asked, "Were you out on the bay yesterday? Wait, I mean, I know you were on the bay but... why were you on the bay yesterday. I'm sorry, but I am really nervous."

Mark didn't answer her question rather he asked his own. "Why are you nervous? You have probably interviewed hundreds of people."

"I know but I never interviewed an award winning journalist. I mean you wrote articles about Jimmy Hoffa, and received a Pulitzer for your work on the Michigan murderer, John Norman Collins. For God's sake, we studied you in college."

"Becca, that was long ago. Now I am just Mark, a snowbird down in the Keys who happened to come across a dead body floating in the Bay. Ask me anything, I'm sure you'll do a great job."

Sherry joined in and told the girl, "Hey, believe me girl, he's nothing special. He spent a few years scribbling for a newspaper and now he writes two-bit murder mysteries. You don't need to be in awe of him."

Mark looked at his wife and questioned, "Two-bit murder mysteries?"

Becca took a sip of her iced tea, arranged the notebook on her lap and asked, "What is your full name and address? It's just for our records."

From that point on the interview went fine, Becca calmed down and Mark was open and forthcoming with his answers, although he didn't really have much to tell her. He told her about seeing the corpse in the distance and thinking it was a sea turtle. He told her he was able to secure the body so it wouldn't float away and held it close to his boat until the Coast Guard arrived. Some things he avoided telling her was that the flesh of the hand peeled off when he grabbed it, that the person was unrecognizable from creatures feasting on its face and the eyes had been eaten out of the sockets, he also didn't bother to describe how putrid the body smelled nor did he tell her that it made him vomit. All details he also had not shared with his wife.

Becca thanked Mark for the interview, telling him it was an honor meeting him. Mark brushed off the complement telling her, "I'm retired and I passed the torch of quality journalism on to your generation. Now it is your turn to protect the freedom of the press."

Phone numbers, email addresses and a promise to stay in touch were exchanged. Mark requested that she call him if she heard anything about the identification of the body, saying, "I would prefer to call the deceased by name rather than the body in the bay."

When Becca left Sherry kissed Mark on the forehead and said. "Well, Mr. Pulitzer, don't let it go to your head. You're just Mark to me."

Mark looked at his wife and responded, "Yeah, just a writer of two-bit murder mysteries."

Chapter Three

Again that night, Mark couldn't sleep. He lay next to Sherry wondering if the body had been dumped in the bay, accidentally fell off a boat and drowned, or maybe he is a victim of Hurricane Irma. "I didn't see any visible wounds that would indicate he was murdered, so maybe it is just accidental or a hurricane related death. But then maybe wounds couldn't be easily observed because the body was so bloated and in such a state of decomposition," he thought.

"I wonder how long he," Mark decided to just refer to the body as a he, "How long he was in the water? I guess I don't know the effect extended submersion in water has on a body. That will be a Google search for someday." He turned over hoping to sleep.

The next morning Mark awoke early and was sitting on their lower balcony sipping coffee as the sun rose in the east. He checked the Keys online newspapers to see if anything new had been written about his floater, the term the Detroit police used to describe a body found in the river. *The Island Times* had updated their initial story with information he provided Becca yesterday. The article gave his name, that he was vacationing from Michigan and that he is a retired reporter with the Detroit Free Press. It went on to say that he secured the body to his boat, called 911 and waited for the Coast Guard from Station Islamorada to respond.

The next few paragraphs related information from an interview Becca had with Chief Petty Officer Terry Kyriss of

Station Islamorada. The Chief reported, "We received a 911 call at 9:37 am, and a small boat crew was dispatched to the coordinates provided; northeast of the Cowpens Anchorage. Upon arriving, our crew took control of the situation from the civilian who discovered the body. After taking a report we transported the victim to the Tavernier Creek Marina where an ambulance was waiting."

"Hey, I was mentioned again in the article. I'm the civilian," Mark smiled.

There was no mention if the body was male or female, whether it was a local, immigrant or tourist, nothing to indicate the authorities had determined the person's identification. "I guess I'll have to keep checking back." Remembering his vow to have a calm relaxing winter and not become embroiled in any crimes, Mark said, "I'm not getting involved, I'm just curious."

Mark wondered what could be determined from the level of decomposition of the body. A quick search on Google provided him with more information than he needed. He found a website based on a scientific study made with pig carcasses suspended in both fresh and salt water at varying depths, temperatures and for varying periods of time.

After reading several pages, Mark refreshed his coffee and got his notebook and pencil. He was going to take notes. "I never know when I may need the information for another book."

~ ~ ~

In his second novel, Mark decided to continue with the serial killer from his first book; Will Mellard. Will is a 25-year-old who lives with his mother, works as a dishwasher and enjoys killing people.

Will Mellard was washing the pots and pans in the kitchen of the Lakeside Seafood Bar and Grill, at the Hawthorn Blossom Resort on Missouri's Lake of the

Justin Maxwell

Ozarks. It's a job he held since his junior year of high school. As he scrubbed burned cheese from an omelet pan he overheard Dianne, the new waitress, a freshman at Central Methodist University, talking with Patty a senior member of the wait staff.

"Mr. Berra wants me to deliver lunch to his office again. Will you come with me?" Dianne pleaded. "Please Patty, please, he scares me. The last time he said, "Come here, let me give you a tip. And when I got close he grabbed me and hugged me and when I pulled away he rubbed his hands along the side of my body. He is creepy."

"Sure honey, I'll go with you," Patty said. "He hasn't pulled that crap on me since the time I picked up the steak knife from his plate and told him if he ever touched me again I would cut his nuts off."

The two women left to deliver lunch to Bill Berra, the general manager of the resort. Will didn't like Mr. Berra, he was mean. He looked down at the hired help, only acknowledging the guests or sucking up to the board of directors.

One time Will saw Mr. Berra around the holidays and wished him, "Merry Christmas, Mr. Berra." The man, dressed in an expensive dark gray suit and red tie, looked at the dish washer, wearing a stained gray sweatshirt and jeans covered by a dirty white apron. He turned away without a word. No Merry Christmas, not a smile, nothing. It made Will feel small, as if he didn't exist. From that day on Will didn't like Mr. Berra, but now that he heard the two waitresses talking he really didn't like him and decided to do something about it.

Will didn't see much of the general manager at the restaurant because the boss had a shellfish allergy and the specialty of the Lakeside Seafood Shack was shrimp. They served shrimp and cheddar omelets, shrimp and grits, shrimp cocktail, coconut breaded shrimp, fried butterfly

13

shrimp, shrimp scampi, roasted garlic shrimp, grilled shrimp salad and the favorites on the lunch menu were the shrimp po boy sandwich and shrimp cakes.

One day Will was cleaning up after the breakfast buffet when the cook placed an Elk Burger with a heaping pile of fries under the heat lights and yelled to Dianne, "Order up."

The cook turned to Will and said, "Tell Dianne, Mr. Berra asked for her specifically to deliver his lunch. I'm going out back for a smoke."

Will looked around. The cook was out having a cigarette with the rest of the kitchen staff; it was their few minutes of downtime before the lunch rush. Dianne was cashing out a customer and Will was alone in the kitchen. He took the opportunity to modify Mr. Berra's burger.

He removed the medium-rare elk burger patty from the bun took it to the walk-in cooler where he placed it in a large pan of raw shrimp. He swirled the pot so the entire burger was covered with the crustacean then pushed down on the shrimp pressing the juices into the burger. When he was sure the burger had been smothered with shrimp he dug out the burger, wiped off the scales and returned it to the bun waiting under the heat light.

~ ~ ~

Dianne, tired of Mr. Berra always trying to grab her, placed the lunch tray on a table in his outer office and yelled, "Mr. Berra, your lunch is in the waiting room."

The boss hollered back, "Bring it on in, honey."

But she had already left. Berra wasn't happy. He got up from his desk, got his meal, shut his door and locked it. He put the lunch tray on his desk and opened a site on his computer, "Girls do it All!" He settled in his overstuffed desk chair for lunch and a movie. He took a bite of his burger and opened a page with two girls alone in their college dorm room.

After a few bites, Berra's breath became heavy, he attributed it to the movie and continued eating as he watched the two young girls on screen. Unconsciously, he scratched a rash forming on his neck. With the next bite he thought his lips and tongue felt funny, but his blood pressure was dropping and his mind was foggy. Once realizing he was in the grip of anaphylactic shock, he quickly jumped up to find his EpiPen. Being dizzy he fell, striking his head on the walnut desk.

No one knew, in fact no one cared, where Mr. Berra was the rest of the day. His absence was enjoyed. His cold, lifeless, body wasn't found until the house cleaning staff opened the office door late that night.

The following morning the police questioned the kitchen and wait staff and the authorities determined Mike Berra's death was the result of accidental cross contamination in the food preparation area resulting in death by anaphylactic shock.

Will Mellard smiled.

In setting the direction for his second novel, Mark wrote that Will's mother was found dead and was determined to be a victim of the murderer who was stalking residents and visitors of the Lake of the Ozarks region. Will inherited his mother's house, the same house she inherited from her parents, but what Will didn't know was that his miserly mother also inherited a fortune from her parents. A fortune which was now his to spend.

Will had three passions; playing games on his old Nintendo 64, passenger trains, and a desire to see national parks, monuments and other popular vacation sites around the country. Unfortunately, his mother didn't share his love of travel and never wanted to go anywhere. In fact, in all her 58 years she never left Missouri.

Will didn't share his mother's penny-pinching ways and decided he was going to enjoy his inheritance. He left his job at the Lakeside Seafood Bar and Grill to travel America and see all that he had read and dreamt about. To begin his adventure, he bought a bus ticket and took off for Kentucky

So far, Mark wrote about his predatory killer hiding in the passageways of Kentucky's Mammoth Cave National Park. At over 400 miles, Mammoth Cave is the longest cave system in the world and offers unlimited locations where his murderer could hide and hunt unsuspecting tourists.

Mark had fun writing about Will seeking out victims and following them through the dimly lit labyrinth of underground passageways. He lured a man into the catacombs off limits to the public and impaled him on a century old stalagmite. The body was left face up, his arms and legs lying limp at its side as if it was an offering to the cave gods. Will scrawled in the sandstone of the wall a message to whomever discovered the corpse; "This will teach him not to beat his wife."

The current working title was "*Vacation of Death*". Although his favorite title was "*Death takes a Holiday,*" but it had already been used. Yet he also still liked a previous title, "*Natural Beauty / Unnatural Death.*" He still had plenty of time to come up with an appropriate title.

Mark was so absorbed in murdering the wife abuser in the dark and dank passages of Mammoth Cave that he didn't hear Sherry get up and come downstairs. She stood on the balcony with hands on hips in mock disgust and cleared her throat for dramatic effect. "Have I been forgotten?"

Before Mark could apologize for breaking with tradition since he didn't have Sherry's morning brew ready, there was a knock at the door. He checked the time, 8:13. "Kind of early for a neighbor coming to chat," he said.

Sherry added, "And the door is still closed," referring to the condo unofficial rule that if the door is closed you're either not home or not accepting visitors.

Mark opened the door and through the screen saw a man in uniform. He opened the door and said, "Good morning Deputy."

The deputy responded, "Good morning, Mr. Daniels. I'm Deputy Radak, we met last winter."

Mark invited the deputy in saying, "Of course deputy, I remember you."

Sitting on the couch in the living room, the deputy said he needed to ask Mark some questions about the body he found.

"Mr. Daniels, last year you discovered a dead man who ultimately ended up being related to a crime and now this year you find a body in the bay. Do you make a habit of following death?"

Mark laughed and replied, "No, believe me I don't look for trouble but it has a way of finding me. Although as a crime reporter for the Detroit Free Press, I dealt with so many dead bodies I was given the nickname, Correspondent of Corpses."

The deputy opened up a small notebook with a metal spiral at the top. He jotted down Mark's name, the date and the location of the interview, then asked, "Tell me about what you did on the day you discovered the body".

"Well, this is our third year wintering in the Keys and this year I decided to bring a small boat down so I could get out on the water and do some fishing. That morning Sherry, my wife, and I towed it to the ramp at Founder's Park in Islamorada to launch. I backed it off the trailer, then told Sherry she could take off and she towed the trailer back to the condo parking lot and I started heading to the condo dock."

"What course did you take?" the deputy asked.

I decided not to take the intercostal, rather I took the shore course, you know past the Marker 88 Beach Bar, through the Cowpens and Toilet Seat Pass to the bay south

17

of Tavernier Creek. I was just relaxing, enjoying being on the water; I saw a stingray and a small shark, then about a quarter mile or so ahead I saw what I thought was a turtle. As I got closer I realized it wasn't a turtle at all. It was a body floating at the surface. The movement from my boat caused the body to drift away so I reached out and grabbed for its hand. And that was a huge mistake."

"Why is that?" the deputy asked.

"Because when I pulled on the hand to keep the corpse close to the boat, the skin peeled off. I let go of it and the disgusting mushy mess dropped in my lap. I grabbed one of my dock lines and got it around the torso and held it next to my boat while I called 911."

Writing Mark's response in his notebook the deputy asked, "How long did it take the Coast Guard to arrive?"

"I don't know, it seemed like hours but they got there probably about 10-12 minutes after I called. They took the body onboard their boat, took my statement and left."

"Then what did you do?"

"I reeked of rotting flesh, I rinsed my hands and shorts and poured water on the side of the boat where I had been holding the body. Then I came here to the dock, sprayed off the boat and showered."

Mark turned into reporter mode and asked, "Have you determined who the victim is?"

"No, not yet. It is a male, that's all I really know. The medical examiner is working on it. We've cross checked its general description against the missing person's list for Monroe County and no one fits. Now we are checking the missing person's reports for Dade and Broward Counties, but I doubt we'll find a match. He's probably a tourist. You know we get visitors here from all around the world."

"Think he could be an illegal immigrant?" Mark asked.

"Maybe, but I don't think so. They usually come in oceanside, not on the bay."

Mark asked, "Do you think it was a hurricane victim?"

"Maybe. He could have been washed off the island and been floating around, but that was months ago and I would think someone would have reported him missing by now."

Mark continued to press the deputy for information. "Did he have anything on him? Like anything in his pockets that would help identify him?"

"No, the only thing in his pockets was a Canadian coin." The deputy flipped a few pages of his notebook and said, "It was a Loonie, a Canadian dollar. I guess some Canadians carry a Loonie for good luck. So maybe he is a visitor from Canada. But we are still working on it."

"Any idea how long he was in the water?" Mark asked.

"No, I don't know but the medical examiner will figure that out. But from the level of decomposition I bet it was a long time. The body was in a pretty advanced state."

Deputy Radak continued, "I would like to take a look at your boat. Is it still at the dock?"

"Yes, but why?" Mark asked.

The deputy stood up saying, "It's just routine. I need to get a couple of photos of it for the file."

Mark led the deputy down to the condo dock where his boat was moored.

"This is it," Mark said, "The Gypsy," pointing to the 15-foot inflatable boat with a fiberglass bottom.

"Nice boat," Deputy Radak said as he used his phone to take several photographs of the boat.

"Why did you get an inflatable boat rather than a flats boat or something else?" asked the deputy.

"Well, it's about 2,000 miles from our home in Michigan's Upper Peninsula to the Florida Keys; from the northern extreme of the country to the southern. So I wanted something that wasn't too heavy to tow for fuel economy. I did some research and an inflatable had the least weight to length ratio."

19

Body in the Bay

The interview turned into more of a conversation about boats. "You know if you were to fill the tubes with helium the boat would be even lighter and you would save more on fuel," the deputy said showing a glimpse of humor.

The deputy continued, "I have a small inflatable, only 8 feet. The kind that you sit on the tube and steer by reaching back to the engine tiller. I like this, you have a center council with a steering wheel and seating and storage."

"I have a 6 horse engine on mine, what size outboard is on this?"

Mark replied, "It's a 50 horse, 4 stroke."

"Jeez, this thing must fly across the water."

Chapter Four

As the days passed, the excitement of Mark discovering the body was fading. He had not heard anything more from Deputy Radak, rarely anyone asked about the corpse he found in Florida Bay, nor had he heard any follow up information from *The Island Times* reporter.

Mark relaxed on the balcony and worked on his book. He was continuing the plot where, instead of just murdering people at the Lake of the Ozarks, the murderer traveled the country killing people. He began writing;

After a ride from Jefferson City, Missouri with a change of trains in Kansas City, Will Mellard got off the train at Milwaukee Union Station. Will enjoyed the meals, the dome car and his private sleeping car so much he decided that after a stop in Wisconsin he would board Amtrak's Empire Builder and continue on across the northern border of the nation to the west coast.

But first he planned to see another of the nation's National Parks on his bucket list; Isle Royale National Park. The 45-mile-long by 9 miles wide rocky island in Lake Superior is located close to the Minnesota shore but within the border of Michigan. It was once an area of importance to native Americans where they mined surface veins of copper over 3,000 years ago, but now it is a nature preserve with no permanent residents and where wolves and moose prevailed.

Will had an appointment on the island to meet a man he had been corresponding with on the internet. A bus transported him from the train station in Milwaukee to

Grand Portage, Minnesota where the passenger ferry Voyageur II would carry him to the island.

"What are you working on?" Sherry asked her husband when she appeared on the balcony.

Mark looked up from the computer and said, "Oh, not much, just getting ready for Will to murder somebody. What are your plans for the day? I plan on writing."

Sherry settled into her chair and sipped the morning brew that Mark had prepared as soon as he heard her get up. She was about to tell Mark that she planned to relax on the beach and maybe go to the store to buy a stuffed animal for their granddaughter, when her phone rang. "It's Mandy," Sherry said.

With Sherry on the phone with their daughter, Mark took a drink of coffee, looking at the beautiful blue water of Florida Bay over the rim of his mug then returned his thoughts to the computer. He re-read what he had written that morning, made a few changes and began writing again about his protagonist Will Mellard on Ilse Royale.

The two-hour boat trip from Grand Portage to the island was a little bumpy and cool with the waves running at 3-4 feet and the water temperature of Lake Superior being 25 degrees less than the air temperature but Will enjoyed the narrated stops along the island highlighting such points of interest as a 400-year-old cedar tree referred to as the "Witches tree", the shallow water wreck of the 182-foot-long steam ship America *that ran aground in 1928 and sank in Washington Harbor and he especially liked seeing the Rock of Ages lighthouse.*

Will's fellow passengers consisted of a family of what looked like a mother, father, and three boys around ages 6-11. The boys, in Will's opinion, required much more discipline than they received. There was a boyscout troop of eleven scouts and two leaders, all dressed in uniform. The island was a popular place for scouts to camp and earn merit badges. *There were 12 hikers all with backpacks, and a short, fat, bald man dressed in a scouting uniform complete with a wide brimmed scout leader's hat and aviator sunglasses.*

The scouts marched down the gangway two by two under the guidance of their leaders followed by the hikers with all of their current worldly possessions crammed in the packs on their backs.

Will followed the short round scout leader. He recognized the man from the photograph he sent to Will during their online conversations and Will knew the man from his photograph posted on the Wisconsin Sexual Offender Registration website. He was the man Will had an appointment to meet. The man didn't recognize Will from their communications because he thought Will was a 13-year-old boy.

Will watched the short round man in his uniform and laughed to himself thinking the wide brim hat made him look like a fat Smoky the Bear.

Onshore, the hikers gathered together sharing the routes they were going to take. All the hikers agreed that they hoped to see some of the island's moose population.

The round man struggled as he carried his bag from the boat dock to the Rock Harbor Lodge. Will stayed behind him but had to slow down twice as the phony scout leader stopped to catch his breath and wipe his brow. As they walked by a troop of scouts, one of the boys asked the profusely sweating man if he could carry his bag. Will watched intently, knowing he would have to intercede if the offer was accepted. Fortunately, the leader just waved the helpful scout away without a word.

The plan for the following day was for the phony scout leader and Will, the phony 13-year-old boy, to meet near the center of the island, off a trail near Siskiwit Lake.

~ ~ ~

Body in the Bay

Will decided not to take the two-hour ferry ride back from the island, rather he opted for the 30-minute flight on a float plane. He didn't want to be on the island when the body of an overweight, bald scout leader was found tied spread eagle between two trees, his mouth duct taped shut, his pants down around one ankle and his large pale stomach hanging over the severely stretched elastic band of his white Jockey shorts...

"Do you want to take a ride to Shell World?" Sherry asked, interrupting Mark. "I saw a little stuffed lobster we can send to Precious," their pet name for their granddaughter. "Then we could go to lunch at that cute little place tucked away in the trees off the highway, oh, what's it called? Its where they had the conch chowder you really liked."

"Oh, its Key Largo something," Mark said then came up with the name. "The Key Largo Conch House."

"Yes, that's it. Oh, I hope the hurricane didn't blow it away," Sherry said.

Before deciding to reduce the stress of his life, Mark might have been angry at Sherry for interrupting his writing and voiced his displeasure with her, but now he simply agreed to go shopping with her.

Sherry said, "Okay, give me a few minutes to get ready."

Mark took what he expected to be at least twenty minutes to write more.

A few days later, a lone hiker ventured off the trail to relieve himself and found the man with a puddle of dried blood beneath his out stretched legs. The man was dead and from the looks of the wounds, the island's wolves had discovered the body before the hiker.

The investigators determined the wolf bites were post mortem and the man had died of exsanguination. He only had one wound where the blood drained from his body as he was tied between the trees. The wound that the man suffered was the removal of his penis with the Swiss Army Knife found nearby.

Will was aboard the Amtrak Empire Builder somewhere in North Dakota when he read on his computer that the body of a Boy Scout leader had been found murdered in the Isle Royale National Park.

"I'm ready!" Sherry said, once again bringing Mark back to reality.

Mark replied as he closed the laptop, "Okay, okay, I'm done, I killed the guy. Now we can go." Mark placed the computer on the coffee table and closed the sliding glass door wall as Sherry stood in the half bath checking her hair one more time in the mirror when there was a knock on the door.

Chapter Five

"Hi, Mr., I mean Mark," Becca said catching herself calling Mark, Mr. Daniels. "Do you have a minute?"

"Hi Becca, yes come in. Come in," Mark said knowing that since he had a guest the trip to Shell World would be postponed, although he was looking forward to a bowl of that conch chowder.

Mark and Becca sat on the couch and Becca started by saying, "I told you I would tell you if I heard anything new about the body you found in the Bay. Well it took a while, almost two weeks, but the body was identified. His name was Andre Levesque.

Mark asked, "How did they finally realize this Andre fella is the body in the bay?"

"The medical examiner did a DNA test but the victim didn't show up in any of the data bases. But Andre's family hadn't heard from him in a while and couldn't reach him so they sent someone down here from Quebec to check on him. They heard about the dead guy and thought it might be Andre and provided a DNA sample for comparison. And yep, Andre and the dead guy are one and the same."

"Well, that explains the Canadian coin in his pocket," Mark said.

"What Canadian coin?" Becca asked. "I didn't know anything about a Canadian coin."

"Oh, Deputy Radak came by and mentioned there was a Canadian Loonie in the victim's pocket."

Becca, not ready to move on asked, "Did the deputy just offer the information about the coin?"

"No, I asked what they found in his pockets," Mark responded.

Becca was writing a note in her notebook and said, "See, you thought to ask. I didn't even think to ask what the dead guy had in his pocket. That is what makes you such a good investigative reporter, you know what to ask."

Mark said, "It comes with years of experience. I always ask the police everything that I think they should know. Sometimes the questions remind them of things they forgot to mention and sometimes things they should check out. Why was Andre down here, a tourist?"

Becca answered, "No he lived down here, ran the jet ski rentals at the Wild Whitecap Resort in Islamorada. It's the place with the two story Tiki Hut on oceanside. It's one of the most popular places in the Upper Keys."

Mark thought for a minute then asked, "Didn't anyone notice him missing? I discovered the body weeks ago."

Becca answered, "Well, apparently he told people at the resort that he was going down to Key West for a while to work on a business deal so he wasn't missed."

Mark nodded his head at her response then asked, "What did he die of?"

"I asked a friend of mine who is a cop and he said he thought the guy died of drowning. There weren't any visible wounds or injuries, but the M.E. hasn't made any announcement yet. She's still looking."

Mark was quiet for a minute thinking about what Becca had just said then asked, "You mean the medical examiner still has the body? It hasn't been released to the family yet?"

"No, because of the advanced state of decomposition the M. E. is waiting for some tests to come back and still looking over the body for signs of trauma. You know, if he was beat up the bruises wouldn't be visible after being in the water for so long.

"Yeah," Mark said. "I guess the body was so bloated and

28

rotting that signs of a gunshot or a stabbing entry wound would be hard to detect."

Becca checked her cell phone for the time and stood, saying she had an appointment she had to run off to. "That's all I know at this time. The body in the bay may be an accidental drowning or maybe he was murdered. I'll let you know if I hear any more," Becca said as she left.

Mark joined Sherry on the balcony.

"Are you ready to go shopping?" Sherry asked as soon as Mark appeared.

"Ah, yeah, in a few minutes. I want to write down some notes," Mark said flipping the pages of his notebook to the pages he had been recording notes about the body in the bay.

"Did she have anything new about the body?" Sherry asked.

As he wrote, Mark said, "A little, the man was named Andre Levesque and he is from Quebec."

"Sounds French Canadian," Sherry observed.

Mark said, "Good thinking," and wrote French Canadian followed by a question mark. The old journalistic instincts took over and Mark began writing questions;

- If the man died accidentally how did he end up in the water?
- Were there drugs in his system?
- Was he alone or are there more people still in the bay feeding the fish?
- Was he on a boat? Where is his boat?
- Did he fall off the boat or was he pushed?
- What kind of boat; power boat, kayak, jet ski, one of those standup paddle boards?
- What was he doing out on the bay?
- Have there been any abandoned boats discovered on the bay lately?

"There are so many unanswered questions," Mark

mumbled as he wrote. It had been months since the hurricane and if the body was a hurricane victim, the sea creatures would have devoured it by now. "I think I can rule out the hurricane Irma theory," Mark said aloud.

"What?" Sherry asked.

"Oh nothing, I'm just talking to myself. How soon before you're ready to go to the shell shop and take me out for a bowl of conch chowder?"

Chapter Six

Will met some nice people on the train. One woman whom he shared a dinner table told him she had a granddaughter who she would love Will to meet.

"She's a genealogy specialist; she works at the library in downtown Seattle. She's a nice girl and smart too. Oh you would love her. Are you going to visit Seattle while you're out west? Oh you need to visit Seattle, it's a beautiful city, it's located on Puget Sound, you know."

Will just smiled at the woman as she continued to talk seemingly without taking a breath.

"The last time I was there Sue, that's my granddaughter, Sue, she took me to Pikes Place. That's the big farmers market where they throw the fish. I'm sure you've seen it on TV. Then we ate at a swanky place on the water."

"Sue wanted to show me where she works so we walked to the library. I tell ya we walked! She walks everywhere. We could have taken a cab or called one of those Goober cars, but oh no, we walked. And it was uphill. I had to rest a couple of times. Sue walks it all the time, she's one of those health fanatics, you know. And she is in really good shape, you should see her, not an ounce of fat on her body. Oh I shouldn't tell you that, but she does have a cute figure."

Will sat across from the woman picking at his Thyme Roasted Chicken Breast. He liked the chicken but he spent so much time being polite and listening to Sue's *grandmother talking about Sue that his mashed potatoes got cold.*

As she went on about her last visit to Seattle, Will imagined meeting the woman's granddaughter; "Hi, I'm Sue, I'm a librarian I assist patrons with research in the genealogy shelves, people looking up their dead relatives. Hi, I'm Will, I'm a serial killer, I kill people who deserve to die. Hey we both deal with dead people, it's a match made in heaven."

While Sue sounded like a nice girl, her grandmother was beginning to drive Will crazy. The woman never shut up. She talked and talked even while shoving forks full of fettuccine into her mouth. Will decided he would ask the dining car staff to change his dinner seating so he could avoid the older lady playing cupid.

A day later as he disembarked the train in Portland, Will avoided the woman so he wouldn't have to explain why he wasn't continuing on to Seattle to meet her granddaughter. He thought, "I bet Sue would be angry if she knew her grandmother was pimping her out on the train to a perfect stranger, and a murderer at that."

"Mark, I remember you said you wanted to go to..." Sherry said interrupting his writing. Once she had his attention she continued, "...you said you wanted to go to Brew on the Bay. I remember last year you said that you wanted to sample some local beer. I think it is in January."

"No, not this year," Mark said. "It was cancelled due to the hurricane. The park where they hold the event is being used to store hurricane refuse before it is hauled to a mainland landfill."

Mark closed the computer knowing that Sherry was done sitting quietly and wanted to talk.

"Do you want to go down to the beach for a while? Come on, you can take your book stuff. You can make me one of those umbrella drinks and we can relax with our toes in the sand. Maybe a manatee will show up or a ray or something. You can take your mask, snorkel and those flippy things and go look for a lobster for dinner. Come on, I'm bored sitting here on the balcony. Let's go. What do you think?"

"Okay, okay," Mark said, thinking Sherry was talking non-stop just like the lady on the train. Is it art imitating life or life imitating art? Mark wondered.

Sherry quickly got into her bathing suit and headed down to the beach while Mark mixed her an umbrella drink; what she called his frozen Pina Colada drinks. As she left she yelled, "See you down there!" But the blender was making so much noise grinding the ice he didn't hear her.

He was just about done when his phone rang. It was Sherry requesting a pitcher of umbrella drinks, the girls were on the beach and thirsty.

Mark emptied the bottle of rum into the blender along with pineapple juice, cream of coconut, fresh squeezed key lime and ice.

While the ice was being pulverized by the blender, Mark cut pineapple slices to garnish the rim of the plastic cups. With the blender making such a racket, he didn't hear Deputy Radak knock at the door.

He shut the blender off and added some cherries speared with toothpicks to the cup of garnish, when the deputy knocked again.

"Oh. Hello deputy, I didn't hear you out here."

"Yeah, I didn't think you could hear my knock over the blender. Having a party?"

"No, just the women on the beach demanding a drink," Mark said with a smile. "Come on in."

"I won't keep you long. I wouldn't want you to disappoint your ladies."

"They can wait a little. They won't mind the wait when they get a taste. I put in extra rum."

Deputy Radak stood at the breakfast bar as Mark

cleaned up after himself.

"I told you I would let you know if I heard anything about the body you found in the bay. By now you probably know that his name is Andre Levesque. It's been in all of the newspapers. He is a local guy, moved down from Quebec a few years ago. He was running the jet ski rental at the Wild Whitecap down on lower Matecumbe."

Mark finished rinsing the cutting board of key lime residue and said, "Do you know Becca Cory from *The Island Times*? She told me the name when your office released it. Has the cause of death been determined yet?"

"Yeah, she's a good reporter. That's why I'm here. The medical examiner found that the victim was stabbed in the chest before he was dumped in the bay. Mark, you've got yourself involved in another murder."

"Oh great! No matter how hard I try to avoid trouble I always seem to be attracted to the under belly of society," Mark said, then asked, "Did the stabbing kill him or was it the swim in the bay?" Mark asked.

"Still not sure, because of the effect of submersion in salt water on his body. He was swollen and decaying and all the sea creatures had been feasting on him. He was a real mess. The swelling hid the knife entry wound and since his lungs and guts were like jelly it took a while to find a puncture in any of his internal organs. I guess the M.E. noticed a nick in his sternum from the knife."

Mark thought to himself, "If the victim had been stabbed in the eyes it probably wouldn't be noticed; the fish eat the eyes out of the head leaving empty eye sockets and the soft tissue of the brain would be eaten or rotted leaving no evidence of a stab wound. I've got to remember that, I could use it in my next book. It might be the making of a perfect murder."

Mark jumped back to reality and thought about the body strapped to the backboard and being lifted aboard the

Coast Guard boat and asked the deputy, "I noticed the body's right hand and right foot were missing. Are they related to the death in any way?"

The deputy said, "From what I read in the report, the M.E. suspects they probably came off as the body decayed, or maybe a shark was munching on them."

Mark was in journalistic mode and asked, "Any idea who would want a guy who rents jet skis to tourists killed? Was he selling drugs on the side? Maybe he was running a promotion, you know like, rent two jet skis and get a nickel bag?"

The deputy smirked at Mark's line of questioning and replied, "No, we didn't have him on a watch list. As far as I know he was clean."

Mark asked, "Any idea how long he was in the bay?"

"The ME estimates ten to fourteen days. She said it was hard to get more exact because of the factors involved in a body in the water; water temperature, air temperature, if the body was in open water or caught up in the mangroves, the depth of the water and the salinity can all impact the effect saltwater has on a corpse. Plus, we have had this stretch of unusually warm weather, much warmer than December in the Keys usually is."

Mark asked, "Where did he live?"

The deputy responded, "He had a condo on ocean side near Harry Harris park; the Ocean Vista Condominiums."

Mark thought for a minute and said, "Jet ski renting must pay pretty well. We looked at a place there and it was way out of our price range."

"Oh, I forgot to mention that Andre Levesque's family owns the Wild Whitecap Resort. They're kinda wealthy."

"Well, I've taken up enough of your time, you have some thirsty ladies waiting for you down on the beach. I just wanted to fill you in on what we found about your body, sort of as a professional courtesy," Deputy Radak said as he walked to the door.

Mark opened the door for him and said, "Thanks deputy for the information. I hope you find the person who doesn't like jet ski rental guys."

Mark grabbed his notebook to write himself notes of the meeting with Deputy Radak when Sherry texted asking where the cabana boy was with the drinks. He quickly grabbed the blender, put the garnishes, some plastic cups and a package of tiny umbrellas in a canvas bag along with his notebook and pencil and headed down to the beach with a delicious drink for the dehydrated debutantes.

Mark poured Karen, Deb, Kate, Sue and Peggy the tropical drink, put the fruit garnish on the rim and added a little umbrella. He was thanked and some of the ladies even hugged him in appreciation for the frozen concoction. As they sipped and talked, Mark settled in a lounge chair and opened his notebook.

He turned to the page with a heading, "Body in the Bay." Originally he was just taking notes about it because he might want to use the facts surrounding the death in a book someday. But now he was taking notes because it was a murder, and he was involved in it. Accidentally involved, but he was a player in the gruesome death of Mr. Andre Levesque.

~ ~ ~

As usual when Mark had something on his mind, he laid in bed with Sherry sleeping at his side and replayed the facts of the case as he knew them. He repeated his vow not to get involved in the death of Andre Levesque, and justified his thoughts as journalistic curiosity. Mark mentally laid out the facts.

- Name: Andre Levesque.
- Andre came from a wealthy family since they were the owners of a resort that took up a sizable piece of very expensive Islamorada ocean front real estate.

- Andre wasn't missed right away because he told people he was going to Key West on business.
- Andre was found after being submerged in Florida Bay for ten to fourteen days.
- Someone stabbed Andre in the chest and threw him in the Bay.
- Between the effects of saltwater submersion, and the sea creatures that fed on him the authorities could not identify Andre until his family missed him and began asking questions.

Mark thought, "These are the known facts surrounding the body I found in the bay, nothing that leads to determining why and who murdered him. I should get up and write this down but I am too tired, hopefully I'll remember in the morning."

Chapter Seven

The next morning Mark was sitting on his chair on the balcony, notebook on his lap, pencil in hand, and a cup of steaming black coffee at his side. He began to write down his thoughts of last night. When he had written all he could remember and added the point that Andre lived in the very expensive Ocean Vista Condominiums, he put down the notebook and opened the laptop.

Mark skipped his normal routine of reading the online newspapers and re-read what he had written about Will Mellard on his cross country train trip. Then his mind quickly slipped into writing mode and he began typing.

Will bought a bus ticket from Portland to Astoria, Oregon. He thought he would start there and go south along the ocean to see the Oregon coast then hop the train back east.

He always had an interest in the Northwest. He had read several books of the Lewis and Clark Expedition and searched the internet for information about the tremendous Pacific Ocean waves that shaped the rugged coast.

Will sat on the bus reading the book he bought at Powell's bookstore not far from the Portland Train station; "Oregon Coast: America's Most Scenic Coastline."

The bus drove a route paralleling the Columbia River as Will read that the Columbia River is 1,243 miles long, and drops from an elevation of 2,690 feet in the Rocky Mountains in British Columbia to sea level where it meets the Pacific Ocean at Astoria.

Will rented a car and took in all of the tourist and historical sites. Astoria is where the Lewis and Clark Expedition concluded their cross continental journey. Will toured Fort Clatsop, a replica of the 1804 fort they built, and anything else celebrating Lewis and Clark's achievements. Will climbed the Astoria Column and keeping with tradition threw a balsawood airplane off the top, then he drove by the Goonie House where the movie was filmed.

He booked a room in a motel that was a converted fish cannery built a century ago. He laid in bed and read a newspaper he picked up in the lobby. There were the usual stories about the city council debating a parking ordinance, a local girl scout troop that won an award for selling cookies, and an Astoria man who was found guilty of embezzling funds from a local business and was out on bail as he awaited sentencing. The man stole so much money that the business was forced to close, putting hundreds of people out of work.

Will said out loud, "This guy is a piece of shit individual, this Dennis Scherman. Because of his selfish greed now hundreds of good hard working people are out of work."

The next day Will climbed aboard the trolley that traveled along the riverfront getting off to tour the Columbia River Maritime Museum. There he learned about the mighty river, it's history and the impact it had on the Pacific Northwest. That evening on a recommendation of the girl working the motel desk, Will decided he would dine at a craft brewery built out over the river on heavy timber pilings.

As he arrived at the brewery, the first thing he heard was the chorus of barking sea lions. The huge California sea lions made the Columbia River their home due to the *abundant supply of salmon to feed on.*

In the restaurant Will sat at the bar with an IPA brewed in the stainless steel tanks just the other side of a glass wall. He watched the social dynamics of the clientele and staff; families with young children, couples whose body language gave the appearance they were on a first date, two guys at the bar whose knees touched as they sat close, and a bartender who openly flirted with members of the wait staff.

There was an area of the dining room with large glass panels in the floor. Beneath the glass were pilings and timbers illuminated by floodlights where several sea lions laid. There were mostly males, almost eight feet long and weighing over seven hundred pounds and a few smaller females. Diners lined the glass floor watching the huge beasts as they jostled for a comfortable berth and barked their throaty call. The enjoyment of the crowd watching a female trying to climb on the timber was replaced with screams as a man's face floated to the surface. The body of a man had been carried downstream on the current and became hung up on the pilings below the brewery.

Will took a look through the glass floor at the body of the man speared by a rusty spike, then returned to his stool at the bar smiling and saying to himself, "Wow, what a coincidence, I'm actually here when the body of Mr. Dennis Scherman surfaced." Then he ordered another beer. He took a sip and thought, "That will teach him not to be so greedy and ruin the lives of good honest people."

Chapter Eight

Hearing sounds upstairs, Mark quit writing in anticipation of Sherry's arrival on the balcony. He was ready; he had her French Vanilla and caffeine potion sitting on the table next to her chair when she arrived on the balcony.

"Good morning beautiful," he greeted her.

She smiled and asked, "So what are we doing today?" She seemed much more cheerful than he expected after she and the ladies on the beach shared two blenders of Pina Coladas.

Sherry continued. "Do you want to take a ride somewhere or go shopping? We could go to that bookstore in Islamorada you like so much. What's its name, something about reading and fishing? Rods and Reading, Reading and Reeling?" she suggested knowing they weren't right.

"Hooked on Books," Mark said.

"Yeah, that's it, we could go there and see what's new. What do you think? I've decided you spend too much time with that computer and have to get out and enjoy life a little."

"I do enjoy life and I enjoy writing. It's my hobby and if that first book sells it might become my new profession," Mark replied. "You know what I would like to do today? I would like to take a boat ride, just you and I. We can get out on the water on this beautiful, warm sunny day. What do you think?" He asked knowing that his wife did not share his love of boating.

43

"Sure, it sounds fun. Where are we going?" Sherry agreed because she knew Mark had not been out on the boat since he found the body in the bay.

Mark said, "I think we should take a nice, slow ride south on the intercostal down to Snake Creek and go to lunch at Smugglers Cove. Are you up for it?"

"I wish we could go to Island Grill and sit on the beach and eat," Sherry said, but the Island Grill was severely damaged by the hurricane and was closed.

Sherry downed the last of her morning concoction and asked, "When do you want to leave? I can be ready in an hour or so. I really need to shower first."

Mark smiled and said, "Take two hours if you want. We have all day."

Sherry mixed herself another cup and went upstairs to shower and Mark opened up the computer.

With a few minutes to spare while Sherry prepared herself, Mark did some research on the stages of death. One site in particular piqued Marks's interest. He flipped to an empty page in his notebook.

In outline form Mark wrote;

Five Stages of Death

1. <u>Pallor mortis,</u> pale appearance to the flesh, happens within 15–25 minutes of death.
2. <u>Algor mortis,</u> change in body temperature after death. It occurs as a steady decline until the body reaches the ambient temperature.
3. <u>Rigor mortis,</u> the limbs of the corpse stiffen as a result of a chemical change in the muscles after death. It can be observed as quickly as 30 minutes' post mortem.
4. <u>Livor mortis</u> – lividity or coagulation. through gravity the blood settles to the lowest point of the body causing a purplish discoloration of the skin.
5. <u>Putrefaction</u> – The decomposition of a body after

death. The soft tissues and organs of the body break down which produces gases that causes the body to bloat.

Mark smiled as he wrote the last stage of death, "I am well aware of putrefaction. I found out the hard way that you don't want to shake hands with a body that is in an advanced stage of putrefaction."

Mark thought for a minute and said to himself, "If a putrefied guy gives you the finger, he literally gives you a finger!" Amused with his jokes, Mark thought of more putrefied body humor.

"What do you call a putrefied guy in a hot tub? Stew!" Putrefied guys make good neighbors; they're always willing to lend a hand. What happened when a putrefied guy ran through a screen door? He strained himself."

"Okay, now I'm just getting goofy," Mark said about the humorous putrefied body tangent he drifted off on.

Mark realized the stench of a rotting corpse had not crept into his mind in a few days and he no longer was haunted by the feeling of the mushy, slimy flesh in his hand. He hoped those flashbacks were behind him.

He closed the computer and began getting the boating gear together. He got out the soft side cooler for a couple bottles of water and two beers, and he gathered their beach towels just in case they jumped in for a swim.

He heard the shower turn off upstairs and hoped Sherry wouldn't take much longer, it was almost 10:30. He regretted telling her to take her time. If they didn't leave soon, the docks at Smugglers would be full. Mark went upstairs to change into his swim suit.

Chapter Nine

When they returned from lunch, Mark secured the boat to the dock and was flushing the engine with freshwater, a task necessary with saltwater boating. Sherry left saying the Coors Light at lunch and the bottle of water on the way back had stretched the limits of her kidneys.

She quickly walked across the beach to the lower commons area where Wendy and Doreen were playing a board game. They asked Sherry if she would like to join them but she hurried by explaining, "Not now, I've got to pee."

As she quickly climbed the stairs, she saw a man tucking a note in the jam of the screen door of their condo. "Can I help you?" Sherry asked, hoping it wouldn't be a long conversation.

The man in a French accent replied, "Hello, I am looking for Mr. Daniels. This is his home, yes?"

"Yes, this is his home but he is not here right now."

"I see, could you please give him this note and ask him to telephone me?" the man said slipping the piece of paper from the door.

Sherry, now in a state of urinary urgency volunteered, "Mark is down on the dock cleaning the boat. You can find him there."

Part of his normal post ride routine, Mark was rinsing the shiny black Mercury outboard spotted by the saltwater. He stopped spraying and was waiting for the bilge pump to empty the collected water and reached for his can of beer in the cup holder. He wiped the sweat from his brow with his forearm and turned the can up for a not so refreshing drink from a beer too long from the cooler.

"Mr. Daniels?" Mark heard. He looked to the dock to find a man standing there. Like any good reporter, Mark quickly took in the man's appearance; brown Bruno Magli leather shoes, perfectly creased khaki slacks, a designer silk long sleeve shirt with a tie that probably cost more than a dinner out for he and Sherry. "Not from around here," Mark thought.

"Mr. Daniels?" the man repeated.

"Yes, I'm Mark Daniels. How can I help you?"

"I am Marcel Lisette; I would like to talk with you about the unfortunate death of Andre Levesque."

Mark listened to the man's accent and thought, "Nope, definitely not from around here." Mark climbed out of the inflatable boat, wiped his wet hand on his tee shirt and offered it to Mr. Lisette.

The two men sat on chairs on the beach, a picture of contrasts, Mark in a bathing suit, Schooners Wharf bar tee shirt and flip-flops while his guest was way overdressed for a warm day on the sand.

The man began, "Thank you for taking time to speak with me, Mr. Daniels. I represent the family of Andre Levesque."

Mark said, "Sure, what do you want to know? And please call me Mark."

"Very well. Mark, the family is understandably very distraught and have requested that I speak with you about the death of their son. Can you please tell me how you came to discover Andre?"

Mark relayed the story of how he discovered the body. About thinking it was a turtle and holding it next to his boat until the Coast Guard arrived. Out of respect to the parents of the deceased, Mark omitted the part about grabbing its hand and coming away with a disgusting handful of slimy mushy flesh.

Mr. Lisette said, "I understand the body of Andre will be less than presentable for a funeral visitation. It has been recommended that Andre's parents should not view him, your authorities told me it is quite gruesome."

Mark said, "Yes, from what I saw the body had been in the water for some time and the immersion had a horrendous effect on it."

"If you don't mind my asking," Mark said, "How did you find my address?"

Mr. Lissette replied, "Your personal data were in the police report. And as the Levesque family solicitor I am privy to the document."

"The family is adamant to find the person or persons responsible for Andre's death. Do you have any ideas as to who would desire him harm?"

Mark responded to the question, "No, I didn't know Andre while he was alive. My only involvement in the death of Andre was finding him after the fact."

Mr. Lisette stood and thanked Mark for his time. He handed Mark a card with his phone numbers and address in Quebec.

"Please give the family my condolences," Mark told Mr. Lisette.

"Thank you, I will convey your sympathies to Mr. and Mrs. Levesque."

The men shook hands and walked across the beach to the parking lot, Mark left the impression of flip flops in the sand while Mr. Lisette left the impression of quality leather footwear. Men from two different worlds.

When Mark arrived at the condo Sherry asked, "Did a guy find you on the dock? He was at our door when I got up here."

Chapter Ten

The next morning Mark sat on the balcony while hot water dripped through the Columbian dark roast in the kitchen. He reviewed the notes he had taken after meeting Marcel Lisette, the Levesque family attorney. Mark thought, "I feel badly for Andre's family. But who murdered him and why, is not my problem," Mark said enforcing his decision not to get involved in anything.

After a career overflowing with death and the murders he unintentionally became involved in the previous winter, Mark resolved to follow Andre's death from a distance and concentrate on the murders of Will Mellard in his next book.

Mark opened the laptop and continued writing about his protagonist in the Northwest;

After the discovery of the greedy and loathsome Dennis Scherman floating downstream and being impaled on a rusty spike of the pilings, Will decided to drive south along the coast. As every tourist should, he visited the wreck of the Peter Iredale, *the four-mast steel sailing vessel that ran ashore in 1906, its skeletal remains sits on a Warrenton, Oregon beach as a testament to the power of the wind, waves and currents of the Pacific Ocean.*

Continuing down highway 101, Will came across the seaside community appropriately named Seaside, Oregon. He joined the hundreds of people walking the one-and-a-half-mile-long Promenade with fantastic vistas of the Pacific Ocean and Tillamook Head to the south.

Will wanted to continued south along the coast but he

51

had to get back to Portland to catch a train back east.

~ ~ ~

Sitting in the dome car, Will sipped a Pike's Place IPA from the train's café car and read a book about his next stop, Mount Rushmore.

Will had long admired the determination and tenacity of *Sculptor Gutzon Borglum who spent 14 years carving the 60-foot-tall heads of presidents Washington, Jefferson, Lincoln, and Theodore Roosevelt from the solid wall of granite. Will was determined to see it while he was so close. He made arrangements to rent a car and drive from the Minot train station to the Black Hills of South Dakota and Mount Rushmore National Memorial.*

"Forgotten again," Sherry said standing on the balcony, hands on hips.

Mark, deep in thought, didn't respond. Sherry dramatically cleared her throat to get his attention.

Mark looked up from the computer saying, "Oh, I'm sorry Hon. I didn't hear you get up. I'll get your coffee."

"Never mind, I'm just playing with you. I'll get it. Want a refill?"

"Sure, thanks."

Handing Mark his cup of steamy black, Sherry asked, "Where were you that was so mesmerizing that you didn't hear me get up?"

"I was thinking of a way to murder someone at Mount Rushmore."

Sherry just shook her head in mock disgust. Mark returned his attention to the laptop and back to the task of murder.

In a rental car, Will joined the parade of vehicles entering the park. He followed the attendant's directions and found a vacant spot in the parking structure not far from the entrance. As he checked the contents of his back pack, Will noticed a family standing at the rear of a gray

Dodge minivan. A girl about 11 years old was bouncing a wiggling toddler at her hip while another child about 6, was obviously anxious to get to the memorial. Mom and dad opened the lift gate of the minivan and pulled a couple of beers from a cooler. The 6-year-old said, "Come on, I wanna go see the rock guys." The dad popped open his Bud and yelled for the kid to shut up.

The dad raised his hand, and the boy cowered, afraid his father was going to smack him with the back of his hand as he yelled, "Dammit, we will go when we're done with our breakfast beer."

Will watched the family from the vantage point of his car. He felt sorry for the kids, the 6-year-old was intimidated by his father, and it looked as if the young girl was forced to be the primary care giver of the baby.

Will watched as the parents opened another can of beer and said to himself, "Some people don't deserve to be parents." He was infuriated with them, especially the father who threatened to slap the young boy.

Rather than continue watching the family and keep getting madder by the minute, Will locked his car, hoisted his back pack and walked towards the entrance.

Mark looked up from the computer when their neighbor Debby yelled, "Good morning, Sherry."

Over the balcony railings they discussed the day's weather forecast; 82 degrees, clear sky and calm winds.

"Just like yesterday and the same predicted for tomorrow," Debby said.

Sherry responded, "How boring."

Mark turned his attention back to the computer while the girls made arrangements to get the other ladies of the condo together for lunch and shopping.

"You don't mind do you?" Sherry asked Mark.

"No, not at all," Mark said, secretly happy Sherry was going to be out of the house for a while since his creative juices were flowing and he wanted to continue writing about Will Mellard visiting Mount Rushmore without interruption.

Within two hours, Sherry had consumed two cups of French vanilla and coffee, showered, and was ready to go with the ladies on a lunch and shopping extravaganza.

"Do you mind if I take the car?" Sherry asked.

"Nope, I'm not going anywhere, I'm going to sit right here and murder someone," Mark answered.

From the second floor Mark waved to the ladies filling all seven seats of the SUV then went back inside to make a salami, cheddar, and lettuce sandwich with extra mayo, which Sherry would disapprove of. Sitting on the balcony enjoying the view, with his sandwich and iced tea, Mark was thinking about Mount Rushmore and Will Mellard.

As soon as Will passed through the entrance to the memorial he was amazed at the sheer size of the sculpture of the presidents in the distance. Looking up to take in their grandeur he ran into the back of a woman who stopped to take a photograph. A man behind Mark ran into him, and like dominos falling a bottleneck was formed at the entrance. Park attendants intervened to keep visitors moving.

Will progressed along the main sidewalk and marveled at the heads of the four presidents. He was overwhelmed with the magnitude of the creation.

He passed by the snack shop and gift store and walked onto the Avenue of flags leading to the amphitheater. Will could feel pride build in his heart as he walked the wide promenade lined by the state flags of the of the United States. But his feeling of overwhelming patriotism was dashed when he heard a man yelling.

"God dammit, Larry Ray, get yer ass over here!"

Will turned around to see the family from the parking lot who drank their breakfast. The young boy had wandered to the side to look at his home state flag of Kentucky. The father grabbed the boy by the arm, nearly jerking him off the ground and in a rage swatted the boy's butt several times in rapid succession.

The father dragged the child back to the family. It looked like the boy was crying not so much from the spanking which he was probably used to but from embarrassment *at being 6 years old and being spanked in public.*

Will was furious, it reminded him of his own childhood and his abusive father.

"*I gotta piss,*" *the father said to his wife. Looking around he didn't see a restroom. As he walked towards a pine forest he told her,* "*I'm gonna go piss in the woods.*"

"*Momma,*" *the girl said, bouncing as she held the baby,* "*Momma, Baby Bonnie needs her diaper changed, and she's hungry and so am I.*"

The woman angrily yelled back at the girl, "*Well, change her, you got the damn diaper bag. We'll find something to eat as soon as your daddy gets back!*"

"*God dammit, where is your daddy?*" *the woman said after waiting over 10 minutes for him to return from the woods.*

The young boy replied, "*Maybe he got the diarrhea.*"

"*Oh, shut up Larry Ray and go look for your daddy.*"

The boy returned finding his mamma and sisters sitting on the grass alongside the Avenue of Flags, the baby at the woman's breast. "*I can't find him. I looked ever where.*"

Fifteen minutes later the woman stopped a ranger and explained, "*My husband went into the woods over there and ain't come back. And it be like a half hour.*"

The girl holding the baby on her hip and bouncing said, "*Maybe he fell asleep.*" *Then turned to the ranger and said,* "*The beer makes him sleepy, don't ja know.*"

The ranger called other park employees and they searched the area but the father of the kids was not found. They suggested the family return to their motel and they would conduct a thorough search once the park closed.

The next morning Will was driving to catch the next Amtrak train heading east, and the days crowd was passing through the entrance at the Mount Rushmore National Memorial, buying souvenirs and watching documentaries of the monuments construction in the information center.

A young girl put three quarters in a telescope to get a closer look at the presidents and said, "Look dad, president Washington has an earring." Her dad gave his daughter, who had an over active imagination, a disgusted look then peeked through the eye piece of the telescope and said, "Son of a bitch!" The magnified view through the telescope revealed that dangling from Washington's left ear was a body ... Will didn't like the drunken abusive man.

Mark's thoughts were interrupted by a knock on the door.

He walked to the door and through the screen he could see Marcel Lisette. As he walked to the door Mark thought, "Apparently Mr. Lisette had been shopping and is adapting to the southern climate." Marcel was wearing a Tommy Bahama shirt, Columbia shorts and a pair of Sperry deck shoes.

"Hello Marcel," Mark greeted the Canadian man. "I see you've caught a case of the Keys Disease."

"Hello, Mark. Ah, yes, my attire, I felt a bit conspicuous. Do you have a few minutes to speak with me?"

"Yes, yes, please come in." As the men walked to the living room Mark asked, "Would you like some iced tea?"

"No, thank you. This is not a social visit. I am here because the family of Andre is quite concerned with the languorous pace of the police investigation. They feel the authorities are not perusing the perpetrator with the necessary alacrity."

"You know Marcel; English may not be your first language but your English vocabulary is great."

"Thank you. I appreciate your accolade. But as I was conveying to you, the Levesque family is not at all pleased with the pace of the police inquiry in to the death of their son."

Mark offered, "Perhaps there is more going on behind the scene than you know."

"Mr. Levesque is a man that demands results. He requires nothing less than perfection from himself and abhors incompetence from those in his employ. And with this inquiry into his son's murder he is not satisfied. Mr. Levesque wants you to investigate his son's death."

Mark looked at Marcel, a bit surprised at his last statement and responded, "Marcel, I was not a police officer. I was a reporter; I wrote about crime."

"I am quite aware of your profession, Mark. I made inquiries into your background. My sources said you were an aggressive investigator and an award winning writer and the Levesque family concluded you are the person they want looking into this issue. You have an extensive past dealing with Detroit crime and an impeccable reputation. We feel with your experience the investigation will proceed to a swift conclusion."

Mark was honored by the request; but it was nothing he would consider. "I want to thank you for your vote of confidence, but I am retired. Now I'm just a writer of two-bit mystery novels," Mark said using Sherry's description of his books.

"Mark, you were an esteemed journalist, respected by the public, politicians and feared yet respected by the criminal element as well. It is your skillset and local knowledge of the Florida Keys that we feel will bring closure for the family most promptly."

"Again, thanks for the complement, but I'm not interested."

"Mr. Levesque is, how should I say this, he is a man who is not accustomed to people telling him no. I will return tomorrow with copies of the police report."

Marcel rose to leave and Mark said, "My answer has not changed, I am not interested in getting involved in this murder."

As he exited the condominium, Marcel turned to Mark and repeated, "You will be handsomely rewarded for your efforts. I will see you tomorrow. Good day, Mark."

When she returned, Mark told Sherry about the strange conversation he had with Marcel Lisette.

"Did you tell him that you didn't investigate crime anymore?"

"Yes, I was very clear that I was no longer in that world and that I had no intention of getting involved."

"I agree; you don't need that kind of stress in your life. And I don't want you spending our winter running around chasing bad guys. We are down here to lay back and live a simple life in paradise."

Mark responded, "I promised you this year I would not get involved with anything criminal and I intend to keep that promise, my love."

The couple relaxed on the balcony, sipping a rum and Diet Coke and enjoying the warmth and fantastic view. Sherry took a sip of her afternoon cocktail and asked, "How much were they going to pay you to snoop around? Not that I want you to do it. Just curious."

Mark gave his wife a glancing look and said in his best French Canadian accent, "You will be handsomely rewarded."

The following morning Mark had barely sat down on the balcony with his computer and coffee when there was a knock on the door. It was Marcel.

"Good morning, Mark. I have brought you a copy of the police report pertaining to the demise of Andre."

Mark, decided to stop this before it went any further. "Marcel, I am honored that you and the Levesque family hold me in such high regard but to answer your request, I do not want to get involved."

Marcel looked at Mark and said, "Mark, perhaps, you did not understand me correctly yesterday. I did not ask you if you would investigate the death, Mr. Levesque has determined that you are the person he wants investigating the death. There was no question, I didn't ask you to investigate the crime, it was a statement. There is no yes or no, you are now a contract employee of the Levesque family, hired to investigate the death of their son."

"We will expect weekly progress reports and of course we will reimburse all applicable expenses." Marcel departed leaving Mark holding an envelope of documents.

Mark stood at the door. He couldn't believe what just happened. Below his breath Mark said to Marcel, "Screw you, Frenchie!"

Chapter Eleven

Mark threw the envelope on the couch and walked to the balcony, opened the laptop and did a search for Levesque. Mark didn't know the family patriarch's first name but the Google search turned up hundreds of pages about a Julien Gaston Levesque of Montreal, Quebec.

As a quick overview Mark selected the Wikipedia page. He wasn't sure this was the man who was apparently his new employer, but he didn't like what he read.

"Julien Gaston Levesque; the head of a Montreal crime family controls the liquor and beer distribution network in the province. He has been arrested numerous times for importing contraband cargo into Canada and exporting it to the United States, but never convicted."

"Shit," Mark said as he read. "I hope this isn't the family that wants me to find out who murdered their son.

When Mark read that Julien Levesque was involved in several enterprises such as motels and resorts, including properties across Canada, ski resorts in the U.S. and a resort in Islamorada, Florida, Mark's shoulders slumped and he said, aloud, "Holy shit, it's him! I'm in the mob! I'm a mobster!"

Mark got up and walked to the kitchen for another cup of coffee but more because he had to walk. He had to think. He had to think about mobsters and murder and things like what mobsters do to people who don't come through for them. No, he didn't want to think about that. But he had to think.

"Maybe with this new direction Mr. Julien Gaston

Levesque was going, investing in legitimate businesses, maybe I've been recruited by a legitimate businessman. Maybe the Montreal mob has nothing to do with this. Maybe he is a changed man, turning over a new leaf, maybe he quit the mob?"

Mark thought for a minute, "No, no one quits the mob. You may retire but you are still part of the mob, you die being a member of the mob. Shit, what have I gotten myself into now?"

"Awe shit. Shit! Shit! Shit!" Mark exclaimed. "I made a decision to not become involved in any crime this winter and now I work for the mafia. I've got to talk to Sherry." Mark made a cup of caffeine and creamer and ascended the steps to his sleeping wife.

After a few minutes Sherry was coherent enough for Mark to tell her what had occurred. He told her that Marcel's offer of yesterday wasn't an offer of a job after all, it was a directive of what Mark was going to do for the family of a mobster. He had no choice, the decision had been made. He was told that he was to investigate the death of Andre.

"What are you going to do?" Sherry asked, showing genuine concern.

"I guess I'm going to ask around and see what I can find out. I don't think I really have much of a choice."

"You could go to the police," Sherry said.

"Yeah, but that might get me killed. I think it would be better if I ask around and see what I can find out and report back to Marcel. If I drag my feet long enough, the police will probably solve the murder and then I'm off the hook," Mark said, not meaning to associate a fishing metaphor with the body floating in the bay.

"Sherry, I know I have told you this over the years, but don't tell anyone, I mean no one, about this. This is serious shit I've got myself into. Deadly serious."

"I know," She replied. "We've been through stuff like this throughout your career and I have never uttered a word."

Mark leaned over and kissed Sherry on the forehead saying, "I know honey, I know."

"Mark!" Sherry yelled after him as he was walking down the stairs. "You be careful!"

Mark sat down on the couch and checked his cell phone, looking for the number of Geoff Henrik. When Mark was at the Detroit Free Press, he occasionally worked with Geoff whose specialty was organized crime.

Mark didn't know if Geoff would even be at the same number he was six years ago when they last talked, but he dialed anyway. Geoff answered on the third ring, "Hello."

"Geoff, it's Mark Daniels."

"Hey, Mark. How are you doing? What are you up to these days?"

"After we retired, Sherry and I moved to the Upper Peninsula and we bought a place in the Florida Keys for the winter. That's where we are now. How are you and Lynn doing?"

"Great, still pounding out articles for the News."

Mark said, "Geoff, that's why I called. I have an organized crime question."

"Sure, what ya need?"

"Have you ever done anything with Montreal crime family?"

"Yes, it's hard not to do anything with the mob without including the Levesque Syndicate. Why are you asking?"

Mark had to think for a second. He didn't want to tell the truth but then he didn't want to lie to a friend either.

Mark responded, "I'm doing some research." Which is true, I'm researching the Levesque family. He continued, "In retirement I'm writing a mystery novel." Which is also true, but not necessarily related to the research.

Geoff told Mark what he knew of the Levesque crime family. They were heavy into trucking and beer and liquor distribution. The family was suspected of using their trucking operation as a cover for smuggling. The old man of the family, Julien Levesque, is phasing himself out, and turning over the day to day operation to his eldest son, Gaston. But when Julien was actively running the family's holdings, he had the nickname of "Sanglante Levesque, or Bloody Levesque."

"From what I heard Julien Levesque has been investing in the States, in ski resorts in Colorado and in Florida. Oh, and I heard that Levesque's youngest son, aw shit, what's his name?"

"Andre," Mark provided.

"Yeah, Andre. That's it, Andre. Anyway, Andre was murdered a few weeks ago. I think it was down in Florida."

Mark said, "Yes, Andre's body was found down here. He was stabbed and left in Florida Bay." Mark decided not to go into details or relate his experience of finding the body of Andre.

Geoff said, "From what I hear Andre was not involved in the family business. He was sort of a different kid. But with the Mafia, who knows for sure. The old man probably pissed off someone or maybe the kid stepped on someone's toes."

The men talked for a while more, mostly about mutual acquaintances from Detroit. Mark invited Geoff and Lynn to visit them in the Keys. A promise was made to stay in touch and the conversation was concluded.

Putting his phone down and said, "Bloody Levesque! Shit! What have I gotten into this time?"

Chapter Twelve

Since Mark was conscripted to work for the Levesque family like an indentured servant and he didn't see any way out of it, he decided he should get started.

First he opened the large manila envelope Marcel left with him. There was a cover letter with instructions that he is to email a report weekly to MBLisette@solicitor.net. Mark flipped the pages to read the police report. He expected his personal data to be redacted but it wasn't. There for the world to see was his name, addresses in both Florida and Michigan, his phone number and even his date of birth and age. "I guess the victim's family attorney gets all of the information."

He dug out a new notebook he would use specifically for this assignment and on the first page wrote;" Andre Levesque: The Body in the Bay"

He transferred all his notes from the notebook where he recorded book ideas; the notes he wrote after meeting with Deputy Radak, Rebecca Cory and Marcel. With all his notes about the body of the bay in one place, it satisfied his need for organization.

On a blank page he penciled in the heading, "Known Facts." On another page he wrote the heading, "Questions."

Since he had more questions than facts, Mark started there;

- Who killed Andre Levesque?
- Why was Andre Levesque killed?
- Was Andre alive when he was put in the Bay?
- Is there a connection between Andre's death and his

father's business? Was it a mob hit?

- What was the business Andre had in Key West?
- Who has Andre pissed off in Florida?
- If his family owned the resort, why was Andre the jet ski rental guy? Why not manager or at least assistant manager?
- Who did Andre associate with?

Mark thought, "There are so many questions about, the body in the bay."

"I like that," Mark said. "I'll have to remember it for a future book title. "Body in the Bay," he repeated.

Mark flipped a page and wrote, "People to interview."

He thought about it and didn't write anything. "Hmmm, where do I start? he thought." "I guess at the jet ski rental on the grounds of the Wild Whitecap Resort."

After lunch Sherry announced that she was going to meet the girls down at the beach. They had been talking about starting a book club and today was going to be the inaugural meeting of the book club named, "The Between the Covers Ladies."

Mark wondered if they shouldn't reconsider the group's name but decided not to inhibit their initiative, although a club logo came to his mind; the members in bed with their heads poking up from between the covers. They could get tee shirts printed with the logo, personalized book marks, heck, I bet bumper stickers would get a lot of attention too. He could have some fun with it. But right now he had other things to work on. He was going to take a ride down to the Wild Whitecap Resort.

The parking lot was packed. Mark had to park near the highway and walk to the front of the resort. He looked around and thought to himself, "It's hard to believe a category 4 hurricane came through here just months ago." There wasn't any evidence of damage. They must have had a crew cleaning up and replanting plants immediately after the storm subsided.

Mark looked around the lobby with walls and floors of polished coral highlighted with lush potted tropical plants. There were bathing suit clad men and women, young and old walking around the lobby, people talking with the concierge about chartering a fishing boat or kayak eco-tours. People still in street clothes were lined up at the front desk, their pale faces evidence of their recent arrival. A young woman in the skimpiest of bikinis covering a very pink body was in the Sand Castle Sundry Shop buying a bottle of aloe to relieve the pain she would be experiencing later tonight from the sun she absorbed today.

Mark walked through the lobby to the courtyard and the crystal clear infinity pool lined with more men and women attired in swimsuits and offering up their flesh to Ole Sole. Guests were reclining on the lounge chairs, cooling off in the pool and those who had spent too much time at the Tiki Bar were loud and competing in a cannonball competition at the deep end.

"Oh, to be young again," Mark mumbled, watching a particularly lithe bodied young woman walk, no, she seductively strutted to the pool knowing the eyes of most men and some women followed her every step.

Mark saw a cobblestone walk leading to the Tiki Bar. He followed the path lined with tropical flowers to the two story thatched roof structure where drinks were served in cups made from coconut husks and plastic souvenir cups in the shape of a south sea tiki god.

The bartender was a muscular, blond Adonis whose looks, Mark figured, were responsible for large tips from the vacationing women down in paradise from places such as; Cleveland, Chicago, Minneapolis and Podunk Junction, Idaho.

"Hey man, whatja need?" the bartender asked, his white teeth almost blinding against his tanned skin.

"Where is the Jet Ski rental?'

"Okay dude, that is oceanside behind the Beachfront," the guy responded as he wiped the bar.

"Oceanside behind the Beachfront?" Mark asked. "What does that mean?"

"Sorry, the Beachfront Burger Bay. It's down that path and to the left. Ya can't miss it. Ya want a beer or something?"

Mark decided walking around with a beer might make him look part of the party atmosphere that permeated the resort, rather than an old retired guy cruising the property checking out all the young scantily clad attractive women.

Another handsome, muscular, blond guy wearing a tank top displaying his massive biceps was standing at a desk under the thatch covered Wild Whitecap Water Sports stand. He watched Mark walk up and asked, much too enthusiastically, "Hey, want to have some fun on the water?"

Mark figured, "Must work on commission."

"Ah, maybe," Mark responded. I was here a few weeks ago and was talking to a guy, Andre, about renting a Jet Ski. Is he around?"

"Naw, Andre ain't here. What can I help you with?"

"I would like to talk with Andre, we were talking about renting eight to ten skis when my family comes down from Marquette. That's up in Michigan. Andre said he was the manager and he could work out a deal. When will Andre be back?" Mark asked

He said, "Let me check the reservation book and see if he left any notes. Unfortunately, Andre ain't gonna be back. He left the company."

Mark thought, "Apparently the company has instructed the employees not to say anything about the murder of Andre, it wouldn't be good for business."

"Really? I liked him, he had that accent. Sorta like a

French guy."

"Yeah, he was from somewhere up in Canada. He came down here to get out of the cold."

"How long ago?" Mark asked.

"Ah, I think it was two years ago maybe two and a half. I remember because I was primed to be the water toys manager but when Andre came I trained him then they made him manager and I got transferred to the Tiki Bar."

Mark decided to take advantage of the talkative guy who wanted to make the commission on the rental of 10 jet skis. "Did you know Andre very well?"

"Yeah, he crashed at my house for a while until he could get in to his place."

"What are you doing here renting water toys if you got transferred?"

"When Andre left, I was the only one on staff that knew enough about jet ski renting to do it. So they moved me back here. I sorta feel like a Yo-yo."

"I bet you would rather be at the bar," Mark said trying to keep the conversation flowing.

"I like this better, it's the day shift. And I still pull a shift or two at the Tiki."

Mark, keeping up the charade to keep the guy talking continued, "Andre and I really hit it off good when we talked. In fact, I was going to introduce him to my youngest daughter. She is a lawyer and wants to move down here. I was going to have him show her around."

The blond guy was more than willing to keep talking, knowing he could make a good commission on the rentals and maybe make a few bucks showing a Michigan lawyer all the Keys has to offer.

"What was Andre like when he moved down here?" Mark asked of his new friend who seemed more than willing to talk.

"Man, when he first came down he was sorta nerdy. But

I took him under my wing and transformed him to a Key-z kind of guy. He grew his hair out, did it blond and started going to the gym up in Key Largo. He turned into a blond beach boy with a French accent that drove the ladies crazy. Ya know the girls down from the snow looking for some passion in paradise."

"So you and Andre hung out together, huh?" Mark asked.

"For a while, but after I moved to the bar we sorta drifted and he started hanging out with Captain Grant of the *"Fishin' Fool."*

"*Fishin Fool*?" Mark questioned.

"Yeah, the *Fishin' Fool* is docked at Marlin Basin Marina, south of here. It's one of the resort recommended charters. I would be glad to show your daughter around, I've been down here since high school, I know all about the Keys."

"Maybe," Mark responded. "I'll get back to you."

"Ah, I don't see anything in the reservation book, what date are you looking at?"

"I need to check, trying to get all the kids together at one time is like herding cats. What's your name, I'll get back to you as soon as I have a date."

The rental guy reached out his hand and said, "Bryce, I'm Bryce." Then he handed a Mark a business card for the Wild Whitecap Water Toys booth.

Mark shook his hand and asked, "What's Andre doing now days?"

"I'm not sure, he was always chasing some get rich quick deal. He is probably in Key West sitting on a yacht sipping a cocktail with a rich widow."

Mark sat in his car in the parking lot, the air conditioner blasting its cool directly on him. He penciled a few paragraphs about his conversation with Bryce, the talkative jet ski rental guy.

He patiently waited for an opening in the endless US1 traffic to drive down to the Marlin Basin Marina to talk with the captain of the *Fishin' Fool*.

He didn't find a boat named *Fishin' Fool* so he asked at the bait shack finding it was out on a charter, "He won't be back till late, they're gonna do some night shark fishing," the bait store manager said. "But here take one of his cards," and produced one from a rack on the counter. "He's a good captain, and he guarantees fish on." Mark added the card to the collection he was acquiring.

Mark thought to himself, "He doesn't guarantee you'll bring home a fish dinner just that at some time during your several hundred-dollar trip there will be a fish on a line." He thanked the man and left.

As he drove back to the condo, Mark was thinking of his conversation with Bryce. "He said Andre went to the gym in Key Largo, I should stop by there on the way home. Maybe someone remembers him."

Mark walked in the gym, a place completely foreign to him, and asked the toned guy behind the desk wearing a tight fitting tee shirt with the Healthy Choice Gym logo if he knew Andre Levesque.

"Yeah, he used to come here a while ago but he hasn't been in a long time. I heard he got killed. Too bad."

The man concluded the conversation when the telephone rang. Mark walked out and was stopped by a guy in the parking lot.

"I heard you asking questions about that Andre guy."

"Yes," Mark said to the man with bulges in his tee shirt where Mark's shirt didn't bulge. "Did you know him?"

"I guess I can tell you this since he is dead. He used to come here a while ago, but he began hanging out with the kids at the gym, ya know high school kids."

At first we ignored him cause, hey it's the Keys, but when we saw him hittin on the high school girls and a couple of them complained we got pissed. One day some of us took him behind the building and "convinced" him to leave the kids alone and to never show up at the gym again."

"I didn't like that son of a bitch. Ya don't fuck with kids!"

Mark asked for the man's name.

He responded, "I'm nobody. It's too bad your friend is dead, but I'm glad he isn't around here anymore." The muscle builder squeezed his large frame into a blue Wrangler with a soft top and no doors. "A real Keys cruiser," Mark thought.

As Mark drove home, he thought, "Andre was harassing high school aged girls. A lot goes on in the Keys that is overlooked but apparently an adult male better not mess with young girls at the gym."

Chapter Thirteen

Over dinner Mark told Sherry what he had learned of Andre Levesque; he moved from Canada a few years ago. He changed from a Canadian nerd to Keys beach bum lady's man. And apparently he was harassing young girls at the gym. Mark then reminded her not to tell anyone what he was involved in.

"You know me; I only listen to half of what you say anyway," Sherry said with a smile.

They went out to the upper deck for sunset cocktails with friends. The conversation was light and enjoyable, a nice reprieve for Mark from dealing with Andre's murder throughout the day. When they returned to their condo, Sherry announced that she was going to the bedroom to watch TV.

Mark settled on the couch and opened his computer. To keep his mind off the body in the bay, Mark re-read the last chapter of the adventures of Will Mellard. He closed his eyes thinking of the next National Park or monument Will should travel to.

The Grand Canyon offers any number of exotic locations where Will could kill someone, he thought. Or maybe Arches National Park in Utah. The park has over 2,000 natural sandstone arches, where a person could fall to his death or disappear in the over 79 thousand acres and die of dehydration.

Working on the book, although it was about death and murder, was a welcomed diversion from what had been occupying his mind.

Mark started typing;

If there was one thing that disappointed Will about train travel was that the clickety clack sound of steel wheels on steel track he expected was more of a clack clack sound as the wheel crossed a joint in the track. And there was no whoo whoo of a whistle or whoosh of steam released from the engine. The age of steam engines was over. But he enjoyed train travel just the same. He could hear the engine's horn blow when they went through a railroad crossing and see the cars stopped at the flashing red lights of the lowered barricades. He loved looking out at fields of wheat and nothing but miles of prairie.

Most of his fellow passengers read a book or used the trains wifi to surf or watch movies on their electronic devices, passing time anxious to get to their destination, but for Will the trip itself was the joy, the destination was secondary. Will enjoyed looking out and day dreaming. His dreams ran the gambit of the waves crashing on the rugged Oregon shore, the majesty of the carvings at Mount Rushmore to the look on the face of the perverted scout leader when he realized he was going to die. And the abusive man at Mount Rushmore and who was relieving himself when Will came from behind, wrapped his hands around the man's throat and squeezed. Will smiled remembering how the man peed all over himself while Will choked the life out of him, a final indignation for the man who abused, belittled and embarrassed his own son.

Mark was tired and his concentration was waning as he wrote about the adventures, or misadventures of Will Mellard. The squishy putrefied hand of Andre Levesque and the disgusting stench of his rotting body began to crept into his mind.

"Hmm, I thought that little trick my mind played on me was gone," he thought. "I guess not."

Mark saved what he had written and said to himself, "It's time for bed, hopefully some poor girl had been sent home without a rose and I can get to sleep."

Chapter Fourteen

Over his morning coffee, Mark checked email. "I'll be damned!" Mark said out loud. "Sherry!" he yelled up the stairs trying to wake up his wife. Then he took the stairs two at a time with his exciting news.

Mark hopped on the bed, almost bouncing Sherry off the other side.

"What the heck is wrong with you?" she asked.

Mark said enthusiastically, "I got an email this morning. Copies of the book have been shipped!" They'll be here next week!"

Sherry hugged Mark knowing how impatient he had been waiting to see his first book in print. "I think we should celebrate. We'll have to go to dinner and celebrate."

He told Sherry she could go back to sleep for a while. It was about an hour and a half earlier than she normally appeared on the downstairs balcony.

Mark refreshed his coffee and returned to the balcony. Mark had ordered twenty copies of *Ozark, Lake of Death* to be delivered upon publication, hoping that those would not be the only 20 sold.

Mark wasn't sure why he ordered 20 copies, "I'll send one to Mandy and my sister then carry 18 back to Michigan."

He regained his seat on the balcony to enjoy the morning and sipped his coffee, watching a three-foot-long iguana in the tree next to the condo. From the second floor balcony he was almost eye to eye with the green reptile. He liked watching the herbivores. Most of time they just laid passively in the sun warming their bodies. Although, Mark read in *The Island Times* that some people eat iguana. "I wonder how they taste?" He thought. Then answered himself with the old saying, "They taste like chicken, but different. After all, they're called the chicken of the tree."

A second cup of coffee and Mark's thoughts moved on from the reptile in the tree to the body in the bay. It was time to send Marcel his first weekly update, but he preferred to wait until he had more information to relate.

At 9:00 am Mark heard Sherry in the shower as he searched his desk for the card for *Fishin' Fool* Charters. He wanted to find out if Captain Grant was going to be around today. He had questions for the captain.

Mark walked into the bathroom and yelled over the sounds of water splashing and Sherry singing "All you need is love."

"Hey, Sher, I'm going down to Islamorada to talk to a guy. Want to go?"

Without hesitation Sherry yelled back, "Yes."

"Okay, but don't take too long. I have to meet him at noon."

As they drove south along the Overseas Highway, Sherry asked, "Is there any shopping where you are meeting the guy?"

Mark answered, "Yes, there is a bait shop. You could check out this year's selection of designer squid and ballyhoo."

Sherry gave her husband a disgusted sideways glance.

"Actually, there is a strip mall not too far from the marina. Remember it's the one with that little boutique where you bought that blue top with a compass rose. I thought I would drop you off while I meet him then we could go to lunch at Lorelei."

"That sounds good to me," Sherry said, then added, "Is Lorelei open, I mean did they make it through the hurricane?"

"Yes, even their twenty-foot-tall mermaid sign on the highway came through without a scratch," Mark answered.

~ ~ ~

Mark approached the man scrubbing down the 34 foot *Fishin' Fool* and asked, "Captain Grant?"

The man looked up, smiled and responded, "Yes, I'm Captain Grant. Wanna go fishing?"

"Captain, I'm looking into the life of Andre Levesque and I was wondering if I might speak with you?"

"Oh," the captain said, disappointed the stranger wasn't looking to book the boat for a charter. "Andre is dead."

"Yeah, the family asked me to look into his death. I heard that you and Andre were pretty close."

"You a cop?"

"Nope, I'm the guy who discovered Andre's body in the bay and a retired reporter. And like I said, Andre's family asked me to check into his life down here."

The captain didn't say anything. He grabbed a long handled scrub brush from a soapy bucket. Mark figured the captain was deciding if he wanted to talk with him or not.

"Yeah, we hung out for a while. Our girls were friends."

"Andre had a girlfriend?" Mark asked. That was the first he heard of a love interest for Andre.

"Yeah, Layla. Andre and Layla were together for a while. We did a lot together, hung out all the time; went to the bars, spent holidays together, went to the sand bar, a couple times we took the boat down to Key West and partied on Duval then staggered back to the dock."

"Is Layla still in the Keys?" Mark asked, hoping to interview her.

The captain, rinsing the deck, said, "Yeah, she works special events, ya know, weddings, business conferences, shit like that at the Ocean Breeze.

"Were they still together when he died?" Mark asked.

"No, they broke up before that but she still had feelings for the guy, ya know. Piper, that's my girl, was over at her house consoling her the night they, I guess you, found Andre."

"Why did they break up?" Mark asked.

The captain thought for a minute and said, "Andre changed. He was always thinking of ways to make a few extra bucks but his ideas started getting a little bizarre. Ya know like illegal shit."

Mark's interest was piqued. "What kind of illegal shit?"

The captain hesitated then said, "What the hell, he's dead. He asked me to use my boat to make a run across the water."

"What do you mean?" Mark asked.

"Andre wanted me to make a midnight run to Cuba."

"For a load of drugs?" Mark asked.

"No, for a load of illegals, you know, people."

"He had it all worked out. The price, the course to follow, the best time to avoid the Coast Guard and he had the contacts in Havana; all he needed was a captain and a boat."

"What did you tell him?"

"I told him no! He wanted me to risk my license, my boat, my freedom, hell, risk my life. I mean doing charter fishin is tough, the profit margin is skinny. There are months I don't make the payment on the boat and there are other times I can make two. I don't make a lot of money but I make it legally. No way I was going to get into smuggling."

"He kept asking and I kept telling him no. I finally had it and told him to get off my fuckin boat and he got all pissy and took a swing at me. He missed and took another that caught me in the shoulder. I pushed him back, just trying to stop him, it was like he snapped, like he went nuts. I pushed him again and he tripped over a bait bucket and fell off the boat into the harbor. I was so pissed that I was tempted to hold his head under but I helped him out."

"Did he ever find a captain to make the run?" Mark asked.

"Don't know. I ain't talked to him in months, and he is dead now anyway. Hey man, I gotta get ready for my 1:00."

Mark thanked Captain Grant for talking with him. The men shook hands and parted company.

Mark texted Sherry that he was done and heading towards the shopping center. She responded that she was near the jewelry store at the south end of the strip.

Sherry was outside waiting when he pulled up, two shopping bags in hand.

As she opened the car door she said, "It was all on sale. And it's not all for me, I bought you a shirt too."

At Lorelei, Sherry and Mark sat at a table on the beach; they both kicked off their shoes and were barefoot in the sand. Sherry swept her feet in a delicate arching back and forth movement smoothing the sand, while Mark's toes dug trenches.

Mark ordered a Spearfish Amber and Sherry an iced tea. "Well, did you solve it yet?"

"No, but I'm finding out things about Andre that his family might not like hearing."

~ ~ ~

Back at the condo, Sherry went upstairs to see if the white slacks and teal top looked as good in her mirror as they did in the store mirror and Mark sat down at the computer to record notes from his first round of interviews.

- Bryce, first friend Andre made in the Keys. Jet ski rental guy, seemed to like Andre, took him under his wing. Under Bryce's tutelage Andre transformed from a Canadian nerd to a buff Keys beach bum. But Bryce was the water toys manager and trained Andre then lost the job when Andre was named manager. Then got job back when Andre died.

- The guy at the gym. – He said Andre was bothering young girls and some guys took offence to it. Some of the regulars took him out back to "Convince" him to quit bugging kids and not to show up again. The guy who talked to Mark said he was glad Andre wasn't around anymore.
- Layla- Andre had a relationship with a girl named Layla. (Parents must have been Eric Clapton fans.) Works at the Ocean Breeze Lodge. I need to talk to her.
- Piper- Grant's girlfriend and Layla's friend.
- Captain Grant- one-time close friend of Andre. Guys and their girls did a lot together. Drifted apart when Andre wanted Grant to carry an illegal cargo. The two argued, punches thrown, Andre fell out of boat. Captain Grant said he was so mad he was tempted to hold Andre's head underwater.

Mark re-read his notes and said to himself, "Hell, with the exception of Layla and Piper they all had reason to kill Andre. He doesn't seem to be a very nice person." Mark wrote down one more entry. One he had been thinking a lot about, a thought that couldn't be overlooked.

- Andre was the son of one of the biggest criminals in Canada. His death could very well be related to the family business.

Mark wondered if he should tell Marcel of his findings yet. How would the family take the information that their youngest son was involved in some illegal activities? Of course maybe they already knew, maybe he was sent by the family to start a new branch of the Levesque Syndicate in paradise.

Chapter Fifteen

Mark drove the palm lined drive into the Ocean Breeze Lodge. He looked around at the finely landscaped grounds with one of the few golf courses in the Keys. He parked in a designated visitor's spot and hiked to the lobby of the main lodge. As he walked to the front desk he stopped to look at photographs of presidents and other famous people down in the sun on holiday smiling while holding their catch of the day.

Mark was very impressed with the opulence of the resort. He had heard that the Ocean Breeze was a chic place where you could easily drop over a thousand dollars a night just on a bed to sleep on.

At the front desk a very attractive and much too perky woman with long flowing black hair asked, "Hello, welcome to the Ocean Breeze Lodge, how may I help you?"

Mark smiled and responded, "Good morning, I was wondering where I might find the special events office."

The perky girl smiled with snow white teeth and told Mark where the office was but said, "Let me call first to see if Layla is in."

Mark was looking around when the girl said, "Layla is busy with a client right now but will be with you as soon as she can if you wouldn't mind waiting."

"Sure, no problem," Mark said.

"You can have a chair in the lobby or out by the beach," she said.

Mark pointed towards the beach.

He walked out of the lodge to the vast expanse of the

blue green waters of the Atlantic Ocean and a wide sandy beach lined with mahogany lounge chairs with monogramed turquoise cushions and matching beach umbrellas. The lodge's dock extended out into the ocean into deep water where Mark could see a boat waiting to take out its days' charter. Like the Wild Whitecap Resort, you would never know a category 4 landed here just a few months ago. I guess if you have enough money you can quickly rebuild even after a hurricane smacks you square on the chin.

He stood there realizing that he might be a bit under dressed wearing Keys casual when a man approached him and asked if he would like something from the bar.

"No, thank you."

"It is complimentary," the waiter replied.

"What? I'm not staying here," Mark said being honest.

"Miss Layla said to apologize for the delay and to get you a complimentary drink while you wait. Perhaps a rum runner, or a hurricane or would you prefer a beer?"

Mark was going to order a hurricane but it just didn't seem right considering Irma had recently called, then considered a rum runner, but felt guilty taking a free drink when he wasn't there to reserve the conference room and dining facilities for a business function. He just wanted to talk with Layla about her old boyfriend.

"Thank you, I would like a glass of water."

"Very well, sir. I'll be right back."

Mark found a wicker chair with overstuffed cushions upholstered in a bright tropical print and waited for Layla.

He watched the guests on the beach and around the pool; kids digging a moat around a sand castle, part of the supervised "Kid Care" program while other kids yelled Marco Polo in the pool.

"Hello, I'm Layla. Are you the gentleman waiting for me?"

Mark looked up at the beautiful blond woman and stood, "Yes. Hello, Layla, I'm Mark Daniels."

Layla reached out a delicate hand to Mark. "Hello Mr. Daniels, how can the Ocean Breeze Lodge be of assistance to you?"

Mark motioned to her to sit in a chair next to his and said, "Actually Layla, I hope you can be assistance to me."

Mark's first impression was that Layla was a woman of class, from her perfectly styled shoulder length hair, to the short yellow sun dress revealing long toned and tanned legs. Nothing like he expected based on Layla being best friends with Captain Grant's girlfriend and the Captain being a little on the gruff side.

"Layla, I'm sorry I didn't mean to misrepresent myself. I'm here at the bequest of the family of Andre Levesque. They have requested that I make inquiries into the death of their son."

The woman's demeanor changed immediately. She was no longer smiling, no longer the vivacious sales person. Mark couldn't read if she was angry that he approached her at her place of work or if she was holding back repressed emotions of Andre's death that still dwelled deep within her.

Before Mark could say anything more, she held up her hand to halt him from continuing. "Mr. Daniels, I cannot talk to you about this matter here."

Mark quickly interjected, "Could we meet at another time and place where we can talk?"

Regaining her professional style, she said, "Yes, I would like to talk with you at a later date. If you give me your phone number, I'll call and set up a time we can meet." She rose signaling the end of the conversation.

Mark handed her his card and said, "Thank you, I look forward to speaking with you."

Mark drove through the perfectly landscaped drive out

of the Ocean Breeze Lodge grounds, passed the courts with men and women dressed in tennis attire hitting fuzzy yellow balls and the golf course with the wealthy chasing dimpled white balls.

Up ahead he could see the traffic on US1 stalled. He turned on the Old Shore Road, a short cut mostly only locals knew about.

The old shore road ran along the Atlantic side of the islands and offered a glimpse of the driveways of the mansions that lined the ocean. All that was visible were the driveways and the landscaping planted intentionally thick so the homes were not visible. "Showing off their wealth inconspicuously," Mark thought. Even the hurricane hadn't revealed the opulence hidden from the road.

"I wonder if Layla will call?" Mark said to himself. "She seemed angry or maybe distraught when I told her the reason I was there. From what Captain Grant said Layla and Andre weren't together when he died, but she took it hard. The captain's girlfriend even went to console Layla when Andre's body was found, when I found Andre's body."

"I wonder how long ago they broke up? And why did they break up? Was he smuggling? Selling drugs, or was he using drugs. I hope she calls, I have a lot of questions for her."

When he got back to the condo he found Sherry in the parking lot talking with Sandi, a neighbor from Georgia. He could see Sherry was either on her way to the beach or retuning; she was wearing her beach cover-up and carrying her canvas beach bag.

"You're back already? How'd it go?" Sherry asked.

"Hi Sandi. Not great, hopefully I'll hear back from her. Which way are you heading to or from the beach?"

"To," Sherry responded.

"I'm going to go make a sandwich and I'll meet you down there. Save me a chair," he said as he climbed the steps.

Mark sat down on the balcony, a chicken salad sandwich in his hand, an iced tea sitting next to him on the table and the laptop on his lap. He opened up *The Island Times* site looking to see if Becca had any follow-up information about the body in the bay.

Chapter Sixteen

Mark excused himself from the sunset celebration when his phone rang. Walking back to his unit he answered, "Hello. Oh, hi Layla, I was hoping to hear from you. Sure, tomorrow at 6:30 at the Whistle Stop, yeah, I know where it is. See you then."

The next day Mark sat on the beach with Sherry and the normal condo crowd and wrote questions he wanted to ask Layla. How did she and Andre meet? How long were they together? Why did they split up? Was he into drugs? Why was he going to Key West? Does she have any idea why and who wanted him dead?

He was sure he would come up with more inquiries as he talked with her but these were the basics.

Sherry said she would prepare an early dinner so Mark could make his appointment with Layla. Mark told Sherry that he could eat at the bar, he reminded her that he really liked the burger the last time they ate there. But she said it was a working meeting, not an excuse to consume a cholesterol laden, carbohydrate filled hunk of beef. He tried to convince her that the pickles and lettuce were vegetables, and the cheese satisfied the dairy requirement of a healthy diet, but she insisted she would cook him a meal.

Mark left the condo a half hour early for the 10-mile ride down US1. He anticipated traffic to slow him down, but in an unusual occurrence, traffic flowed and he arrived 15 minutes early. Mark sat at a table facing the door and ordered a beer. He liked the atmosphere at the Whistle Stop, it was a local's bar with a few tourists sprinkled in for entertainment.

Mark, like most men in the bar, noticed Layla walk in. She had that quality about her that when she entered a room heads turned. Mark saw the striking blond, wearing short cut off jean shorts with long tanned legs walk in before he realized it was her.

Layla was with another woman and Captain Grant. The other woman turned out to be Piper, Grant's girlfriend and Layla's best friend. Grant grabbed a chair from another table and introduced Piper.

Before Mark could open his notebook and begin asking his questions, Grant started in. "We want to know who you are and why you're asking questions about Andre."

Mark was surprised at the aggressive tone of Grant's voice; he was nothing like that the day Mark was talking to him. Then he seemed to Mark to be cautious in his answers but today his attitude was hostile.

Mark was put on the defense, not something he was accustomed to. "I'm Mark Daniels. I live down here during the winter. It was I who found Andre's body in the bay. His family found out that I'm a retired investigative reporter and asked, or shall I say, insisted, that I look into his death. I first talked to Bryce at the Wild Whitecap Resort. He told me Andre worked out at the Healthy Choice Gym so I went there. Bryce also said that you," Mark said looking at the captain, "were good friends. So I went to talk to you. You told me about Layla so I went to see her and that's how we got to where we are now."

The waitress delivered four beers and the two women and Captain were conspicuously quiet while she was at the table. When she left, Grant said, "It's a small island, all of us locals know each other and each other's dirty little secrets."

Mark noticed that so far Layla had not spoken a word. He turned to her and asked, "I hope I didn't upset you when

I went to the Ocean Breeze to talk with you, but I didn't have any other way to get in touch with you."

"Never go there again," she admonished him.

"I won't, I apologize if I caused you any trouble."

Grant asked, "And what have you found out about Andre?"

"I know that you and he had a dispute which lead to you guys no longer hanging out and the dispute was about him wanting you to carry a certain cargo. I heard that Andre," Mark stopped as the waitress asked if they wanted anything to eat.

When she left Mark continued, "I heard that he was suspected of harassing high school aged girls at the gym and was asked to leave."

The three sat quietly sipping their drinks and listening. Mark decided to try to draw them out and get some answers.

"I heard that Andre was involved in something in Key West, what was that all about?"

Grant answered for the group, "We don't know."

Mark turned to Layla and asked, "How long were you and Andre together?"

Grant began to answer but Layla interrupted him saying, "I can speak for myself."

"I met Andre at the Wild Whitecap. I was working there when he moved down from Canada. I think it was his accent that attracted me. At first I thought he was involved with Bryce, ya know living with him and all, and it's no secret that Bryce likes the boys. But we hit it off and started hanging out after he moved out of Bryce's place."

"Was Andre involved with Bryce in a romantic way or were they just sharing an apartment?" Mark asked.

Layla answered, "He said he was just using Bryce for a place to stay, but Bryce was really pissed when Andre moved out. They were seen yelling at each other one day at the toys booth."

"What do you think?" Mark asked Layla.

"It wouldn't surprise me, if Andre and Bryce were an item. Andre had a varied sexual appetite."

Mark wanted to write some notes but didn't want to disturb Layla once she began talking.

Mark asked, "How long were you and Andre together?"

Layla looked at Piper and said, "I don't know, what do you think Pipe?"

Piper said, "I started working at the Whitecap about two and a half years ago and you weren't with him then. I don't know, maybe two years ago."

Mark noticed, "That's the first Piper had spoken."

"Yeah, that's what I was thinking too," Layla said.

"When did you break up?"

"We were off and on for much of the time we were together but I called it quits a couple of months ago," Layla answered.

Mark took the opportunity to ask something he really wanted to know, "What led to your break up?"

Layla looked to Piper then to Grant, as if she was looking for their approval to continue answering the questions.

Piper shrugged her shoulders and the captain said, "It's up to you."

Layla looked at Mark and said, "It is because of the Kasie and Chris Berry wedding. They were getting married at the Ocean Breeze and she was one of those brides from hell. She kept making changes, the day before the wedding she invited additional guests, people she just met on the beach, and changed the reception seating. I took home the file for her wedding to retype the seating diagram. The next morning, I forgot the file.

I couldn't get away to pick it up so I called Andre and asked if he could go to my place and get the file and bring it to me. I waited for him and he didn't show, so about noon I ran back to my apartment to get it. When I opened my door I found Andre and Tennille Gonzales screwing in my kitchen. He was nude standing on the footstool and Tennille had her fat ass on my countertop. I put my food on that countertop! Well, I used to put food there."

Mark noted that the more she talked the angrier she seemed to become. It was an old wound reopened.

"I was so mad I could have killed him. He brought that slut from the Whitecap to my house to fuck. He was lucky my pistol was in my car or I would have shot him right there and probably shot the bitch too."

Mark asked, "What did you do?"

"First I started screaming and threw my keys at him, I grabbed the TV remote and threw it, then a coffee cup."

"Did you hit them?"

"No, I missed them miserably."

"What did they do?" Mark asked.

Layla continued, "Tennille was pulling up her plus size red thong and jeans and Andre was apologizing and telling me he loved me and grabbing his clothes. I picked up a big conch shell to throw and he ran towards the door pulling on his pants. They ran out and finished getting dressed in the hall."

Mark asked, "That's when you broke up?"

"No, a couple of days later. It sounds funny but I still loved the jerk. I hated him, but loved him."

"He kept calling and begging for me to take him back. One day he was in the Ocean Breeze parking lot when I got off work and he was crying and begging for me to take him back. That was it. Him coming to my place of work and embarrassing me was it. I was so pissed at him I wanted to run him over with my car. He was pathetic."

"So, did he leave you alone?" Mark questioned.

Layla smiled and looked at Grant then replied, "No."

Grant said, "That's where I come in. I caught up with Andre and told him to leave her alone."

Mark looked at Grant and asked, "That was it, he just agreed to leave Layla alone?"

"No, we ended up getting into it at his condo and after a few punches he said he would quit bugging her. He was a fuckin wimp," Captain Grant said.

Mark thought for a moment and asked, "Did you stab him?"

"What? No, I bloodied him, but just with my fists. I didn't kill him. Don't put that on me."

"Do any of you know who wanted Andre dead?" Mark asked.

Grant was first to answer, "Andre use to brag that his dad was some big mobster and he ran the mafia and shit back in Canada. I bet Andre getting murdered had something to with his family."

Since Piper was reluctant to volunteer any information, Mark specifically asked her, "Piper do you know of anyone who wanted Andre dead?"

"No. I mean he pissed off a lot of people but not to the point that they would murder him. Except maybe, JJ." She turned to look at the others. "Remember JJ was pretty mad at Andre when he got him fired from Whitecap."

Mark opened the notebook sitting in front of him and asked, "Alright, who is JJ."

Layla started for the group. "JJ worked as a bartender at Whitecap. Good looking guy about 28."

"Very good looking, with a great southern accent," Piper added.

Layla laughed at her friend, "Yeah, you always had a thing for JJ. Anyway, he was great with the female customers. He had this charming charismatic way about him that the ladies loved. Older women wanted to take him home and mother him and the younger ones wanted to jump his bones. But all he did was flirt with them, he never took any of them to bed."

"Why not," Mark asked.

Layla answered, "Because he is married. And I mean really married, with two kids."

"Why did Andre get him fired?" Mark asked.

"I think he was jealous of the attention JJ got," Captain Grant said.

Mark noticed that Grant had been quiet since JJ's name came up and since Piper seemed so talkative about the good looking bartender. Maybe there was a bit of jealously?

"Why is that, Grant?" Mark wondered.

"I don't know. Andre would always bitch about how the girls would fall all over JJ trying to get his attention."

"One day Andre went to Mr. Clark, the resort manager and got JJ fired," Layla said. "He made up some story of seeing JJ with one of the rich guests going in her motel room. It was all bullshit, but Andre was the owner's son and Mr. Clark wanted to keep the owner happy, so he fired JJ."

Mark was jotting down notes and asked, "What is JJ's name? His real name, I assume JJ are his initials."

Piper answered, "Jimmy John James from Jeffersonville, Kentucky."

Mark wrote while he said, "It should have been JJJ."

Piper agreed but said, "I know, but he went by JJ."

"What ever happened to JJ?" Mark questioned.

Piper answered, "He got a job tending bar down in Key West at Sloppy Joes or Hogs Breath, one of those places where he makes a lot more in tips. And his wife is an accountant and she got a good job too. They're doing well."

Grant shook his head in agreement. "Yeah, JJ was pretty mad at Andre but I don't think he would hurt Andre, hell, I don't think he would kill a fly."

Grant continued, "Now Tommy was mad enough at Andre to kill him."

Mark quickly wrote down the name. "What's Tommy's last name?"

"Minor, Tommy Minor. He and Andre worked together at the Water Toys concession for a while. They were friends, but not close buddies. Tommy wanted to be a flats boat captain. He saved every penny he could to buy a boat," Captain Grant told Mark. "I mean he would skip meals just to save a few bucks."

"Anyway, he finally got enough money for a down payment on an old 18-footer, man it was his prized possession. But he was so broke after buying the boat he couldn't afford to put gas in it. One day, Andre said he would fill it up if he could borrow the boat for an afternoon. He had a girl he wanted to take out."

Mark interjected, "And Tommy just let him take his baby?"

Grant answered, "Yeah, Andre could be quite persuasive when he waved his daddy's money around. And Tommy needed money. Anyway, Andre ran Tommy's boat into a buoy on Hawks Chanel. Ya know one of those ten-foot-tall buoys, and on a clear day too. Andre was okay but the boat sunk. Andre refused to pay Tommy for the boat, he said it wasn't his fault."

"Tommy didn't have any insurance and he lost everything. One night at the Ocean View bar, Andre walked in and when Tommy saw Andre he screamed, "You fucker you ruined my life!" Then he started throwing punches, I mean it took three of us to pull him off Andre. Tommy wanted to kill him. The cops came and arrested Tommy, and we never saw him again."

Mark flipped a page in the notebook and said, "It seems like Andre had a lot of enemies. Anyone else to add to the list?"

Layla said, "Don't think so."

Captain Grant shook his head no.

Piper, who hadn't spoken much, said "No, nobody except the Russians."

"Russians? What Russians?" Mark said surprised.

Layla responded, "Oh, Andre said he was going into business with some Russians in Key West."

Grant added, "He was talking about it but I warned him I thought he was out of his league dealing with them. They are pretty bad people."

"Do you know who he was talking with in Key West? A name possibly?" Mark asked, pencil posed to record it.

Layla answered, "No, but I think I might have something at my apartment. He left some papers I was going to return to him, but... he died."

Mark tried to hide his excitement at the possibility of the death of Andre taking on an international intrigue and said, "It might be very important in solving Andre's murder if you can get me those papers."

"Okay, I think I know where they are, I don't think I threw them away. I'll look when I get home and give you a call," Layla told Mark.

Mark told the group, "I think it would be a good idea if we all exchanged phone numbers so we can keep in touch." He pulled out his wallet and produced three business cards with his information and passed them around the table. Grant padded his pockets looking for a card. Mark said, "Grant, I've got your card, I picked up one at the marina. The girls wrote their numbers on a cocktail napkin and gave it to Mark.

Within an hour of returning home, Layla called with some information she found as promised.

"Give me a minute to get a pencil and paper," Mark said turning to a fresh page in his notebook. "Okay, I'm ready." Mark listened and said, "Wait, can you spell that?" Mark repeated each letter as Layla spelled out the first and last name, then read the name, "Yaakov Chaykovsky"

"Do you have a phone number or address?" Mark asked.

"No, but there is a description of the store," Layla answered.

Layla read the description and Mark repeated it to her as he wrote, "Duval, near Mallory, west side, green building, everything $5.00. Okay, I should be able to find it. In fact, I think I was in that shop last year."

"Thanks Layla. I'll let you know what I find out." Mark hung up, reread his notes and said to himself, "Well, Mr. Yaakov Chaykovsky. I hope to see you soon."

Chapter Seventeen

Mark was sitting on the balcony enjoying his coffee and re-reading the notes he wrote after meeting with Layla, Piper and Captain Grant. He looked up and stared out at the blue waters of Florida Bay. A sailboat was at anchor offshore with its mooring lamp still illuminated in the dim morning light. But his early morning revelry was interrupted when his cell phone rang.

It was too early for a sales call about signing up for a credit card or new windows for their house so Mark answered hoping it wasn't anything about their daughter. She drove 20 miles each morning to work and the Weather Channel told Mark the roads in mid-Michigan were icy.

"Hello?" Mark asked.

"Good morning, Mark."

The French Canadian accent was unmistakably.

"Hello, Marcel."

"Mark, I have not heard from you since last we spoke. Have you commenced with the investigation into the death of the son of our employer?"

Mark noticed he emphasized the word "our".

"I'm sure based on your reputation, you have undoubtedly researched your current patron, Julien Levesque. And you are now well aware that he is one whom you do not want to disappoint."

"Hold on Marcel, I've got some questions for you," Mark said, taking an assertive roll.

In a calm measured voice Marcel responded, "Yes, Mark. What is your inquiry?"

"Why do you want me looking into Andre's murder? The police are checking it out."

"Yes, it is true the police are investigating the incident, but the Levesque family has an intrinsic cynicism of the authorities. They do not believe the constabulary will perform an acceptable pursuit for the person or persons responsible for Andre's demise."

Mark asked, "Why wouldn't they? The police want the crime solved too."

"They feel the police will be less than tenacious in their desire to solve the crime based on the unsubstantiated reputation of the family. They might simply determine the situation is the result of a person with resentment towards the family business, someone who may perceive they were in some way aggrieved in a transaction with the family."

"Thus, they determined, based on a background check that you would provide them with an honest, thorough investigation untainted with biases nor preconceived opinions."

Mark asked the question he had been thinking about since he found out about Andre's lineage. "Marcel, how do we know the murder wasn't committed by a person with a grudge against the Levesque family?"

"You do not need to pursue that avenue of the investigation. We already have people here investigating from that perspective. And If we determine a person on our end is accountable for the death, we will deal with it. I want you to concentrate on suspects down there in the Keys."

Mark thanked Marcel for his honest answer and said, "I have made some initial inquiries..."

Marcel interrupted Mark saying, "Please submit your report as an email to the address as instructed."

Mark typed an email to Marcel about meeting Bryce at the Wild Whitecap Resort. That Bryce let Andre stay with him for a while until his condo was available. He did not tell

Marcel of the unsubstantiated relationship the two are rumored to have shared.

He told Marcel of his conversation with a man at the health club. Mark thought the news that Andre was possibly trying to seduce young girls would be upsetting to the family but he had to be honest. Mark next brought up Captain Grant and the one-time close relationship they had and the way the two men disagreed over the smuggling of illegal immigrants and that the two guys eventually parted ways.

Next he wrote the solicitor about meeting Andre's girlfriend Layla and her friend Piper. Mark included Layla finding Andre with another woman, but not quite as graphically as the story was related to him.

Mark concluded the message and pushed send.

Chapter Eighteen

The following morning Mark awoke earlier than usual. He couldn't take up residence on the balcony as he did every morning, since it was still dark out, he got a cup of coffee and settled in on the couch.

He thought, "I need to take a break from Andre Levesque. I was thinking about his murder as I lay sleepless last night and it was my first thought this morning. I need a break." He turned on the laptop and opened the file of his new book. He didn't re-read the last chapter as he often did, he just began typing the words that were rattling around in his head.

After a few weeks at home in Lake of the Ozarks, Will Mellard took the Amtrak to the heart of the United States, Washington D. C. He hoped to find one of the politicians who had been found guilty of sexually harassing a colleague or one who sold out their constituents and integrity for greed and political power.

Will had planned how he would make them pay for their misuse of the public trust. He figured he would leave their dead body floating in the Lincoln Memorial Reflecting Pool, giving the politicians something to reflect on.

Patriotism swelled in his chest as he toured Washington's Monument, the Lincoln Memorial, the World War ll and Korean War Memorials and the Viet Nam Memorial Wall, but the museum that made a lasting impact on him was the United States Holocaust Memorial Museum. Will left the museum in deep despair, questioning how humanity could treat its fellow man with such callous disregard. He wondered how a country could be so easily swayed to discount the lives of others by a sick and demented leader and willingly kill millions of people just because of their religious or ethnic heritage.

From DC, Will took the Silver Star- Palmetto train south to Miami. He was looking forward to the sun and warmth of south Florida since most of America was in the grips of an arctic cold front that brought below zero temperatures, brutal wind chill readings and mountains of snow. Unfortunately, the cold weather had dipped into the south as well. The night time temperatures dropped into the twenties and low thirties over much of the sunshine state, even in Miami. The manatee were seeking the warm waters of the power plant discharge ponds, locals broke out their long pants, winter coats and stocking caps, fish who lived in tropical waters were dying in the now cooler waters of the Gulf. Even the iguana were freezing and falling from the trees.

Will had bought jeans and a hooded sweatshirt in D.C. since he hadn't packed many cold weather clothes for the trip; mostly tee shirts and shorts. But despite the unseasonably cold weather Will was determined to make the best of the South Florida leg of his vacation.

He saw a crowd gathered in a public park not far from South Beach. As he wandered towards the group, Will saw a man with a microphone standing before the crowd, his right arm raised with his hand extended straight yelling "Sieg Heil." The man was flanked by two heavily tattooed men wearing swastika arm bands and other Nazi symbolism.

Will listened to the man spout his hateful rhetoric, blaming all the ills of America on the ethnic and religious groups he opposed. A couple of people cheered, but most others in the crowd screamed back shaking their fists at the hate monger. Three police officers watched the crowd from a distance.

Will thought that the man should realize the very fact that he was allowed to speak his opinion publicly, no matter how despicable and unreasonable, was a hallmark of our constitution. In America, one can have and can speak their opinion, unlike under dictatorships around the world including the Nazi regime where an opinion against the ruling party often resulted in detainment or death.

The man concluded his speech and the group dispersed. The two guards took off their armbands and anything identifying them as Nazi's then left. The police stayed for a few minutes longer then departed, leaving the speaker to pack away his sound equipment and pick up the pamphlets he handed out, which were mostly thrown to the ground. In the clearing of the park all that remained was the orator of hate and a serial killer standing unseen in the woods.

As the man who spoke of cleansing the white race of the filth of other ethnic groups and religions carried his equipment through the woods to the parking lot, Will stepped forward to confront him.

"What makes you think you are so much better than others?" Will asked truly wondering.

The man stopped along the secluded short cut to the parking lot and replied, "Because whites are superior in the eyes of the lord. Those people by virtue of their race and religion are substandard and they are denigrating the majesty of the white race."

Will recalled touring the Holocaust Museum in Washington D. C. just days ago. The images of men, women and children in concentration camps being forced into the gas chambers and the photographs of bodies heaped in piles filled Will's mind.

The man began to shout his racial dialogue at Will,

saying the tide is shifting in America and began calling Will disparaging names and claiming, "It is our responsibility to rise up and save America from the Hebes, niggers and spics."

The man's vile language and the memory of the Holocaust Museum boiled within Will and, in a rage, he picked up the closest object with any heft and brought it down on the head of the Nazi racist.

A day later the Miami Herald printed a small article buried deep in the second section of a Neo Nazi extremist found dead. The police theorized the extreme cold snap resulted in an iguana freezing to death, falling from a tree and landing on the Nazi's head. A dead iguana laid near the body and iguana scales were found in the victim's head wound. Will smiled.

Shortly after filling his third cup of coffee and sitting back down, an email notification appeared on the bottom of Mark's computer screen. Mark said to himself, "You've got mail", reminiscent of the 1998 movie.

Marcel responded to Mark's report with a simple and abrupt reply, "Received."

The reply was short but enough to shift Mark's train of thought from the novel back to the death of Andre. He set aside the laptop and his clever murdering main character and opened a notebook.

Mark reviewed the notes about the murder of Andre Levesque and thought that it sounded like everyone wanted him dead at one time or another. If Bryce was romantically involved with Andre and Andre broke it off, then Bryce might have a reason to do Andre harm. I think it was Layla who said he and Andre were seen having an argument.

"Then the guys at the gym took Andre aside for messing around with school aged girls. According to the muscle bound man in the parking lot, they threatened Andre to stop harassing the girls and not to show up at the gym again.

Then there was Grant who argued with Andre and said he was tempted to hold his head under water when Andre tried to convince him to smuggle Cuban refugees to the United States which resulted in a scuffle and Andre in the harbor.

Then again Layla admitted that Andre was lucky she didn't have her pistol when she caught him screwing the girl on her kitchen countertop or she would have shot him right then and there.

Hell, they all wanted him dead, any one of them could have killed him. And now I need to check out this JJ guy who Andre got fired from the Wild Whitecap, a Russian who Andre had some business dealing with and another suspect named Tommy, who claimed Andre destroyed his boat, his dreams and his life.

Mark was still sitting on the couch when Sherry came downstairs about 8:45. Sherry looked out the door wall and saw nothing but sun filled blue sky, palm trees gently swaying and with a glance at the thermometer which read 76, she asked, "What's the matter, too much paradise outside for you?"

Mark set aside his notebook, and said, "I woke up before sunrise and got absorbed and never made it out. I'll get us coffee and meet you out there."

They sipped their brews on the balcony and Mark asked, "Would you like to go down to Key West?"

"Sure, when? I can be ready in fifteen minutes."

Mark smiled at his wife's response. "Take your time. I was thinking of leaving around 10:30. I have a couple of guys I would like to interview down there if I can find them. So you might be by yourself for a while. Do you think you can find something to do?" he asked facetiously, knowing Duval Street was a mile and quarter long and lined on both sides with shops where Sherry could do some damage to the Visa.

"And," Mark said, "I'm on the clock, so I can turn in the cost of the trip to Marcel as a business expense."

As they drove along US1 Mark said to Sherry, "Hurricane Irma must have changed the vacation plans of some people, the traffic seems lighter than in years past." Sherry added, "And there are vacancy signs at a lot of motels and resorts."

Before the storm struck on September 10, 2017, traffic on US1, the only road between the mainland and Key West, often became snarled with maddening traffic jams and arriving at Key West without a room reservation resulted in sleeping in the car.

Mark relayed some of the hurricane Irma information he had read, "The storm crossed the Keys and 90% of the homes and commercial buildings reported some damage, of them 65% of the structures sustained significant damage, and 25% of them were completely destroyed."

"Why is there still garbage along the highway?" Sherry asked looking at the piles of hurricane related debris. "The storm was months ago."

"I don't know. You would think it would have been cleaned up by now," Mark answered.

Mark looked at a ten-foot-tall pile of debris, containing lumber, tree limbs, tires, furniture, clothes, appliances, child toys, parts of a jet ski and the remains of trailer homes. Mark said, "Just months ago, all this stuff made up people's lives. Now their hopes and dreams are piled in a heap along the highway waiting for a truck ride to a landfill."

Sherry asked, "But Key West wasn't damaged, was it? I read that Key West came out of the storm relatively unscathed."

"Earlier forecasts had the hurricane making landfall in the northern Keys, up by us, then the forecast was for it to hit Key West then turn back and run up the east coast but it changed its course again and slammed into the lower Keys north of Key West and went up the Gulf coast of the mainland."

Sherry said, "Peg, the lady who lives in our basement said the debris piles used to be the height of a two or three story building. I guess they are making progress anyway."

Mark looked at Sherry and said, "Peg doesn't live in our basement, she lives in the condo below ours."

Sherry smiled at her little joke.

The damage was noticeably worse the more south they drove along US1. The most severe impact of the storm was felt below the Seven Mile Bridge to about 15 miles north of Key West near Big Coppitt Key. Business signs were blown away, plywood covered windows of shuttered buildings, the palm trees and mangroves looked scrawny, their leaves and fronds blown off by the winds but were now starting to grow back. "Nature revitalizing itself," Mark thought.

Sherry did a search on her phone and read to Mark; "Hurricane Irma was the most powerful Atlantic hurricane in recorded history. It was a Category 5 storm when it made landfall on Barbuda. Its winds were 185 miles per hour for 37 hours. That's longer than any storm ever recorded."

"Yeah, the storm weakened to a Cat 3 but increased to a Cat 4 when it smashed into the Keys," Mark said.

As they drove over the Kemp Channel Bridge, Mark said, "This is Cudjoe Key, the area of the Keys where the center of the storm made landfall. This area took the full brunt of the hurricane. Can you imagine being here when sustained winds in excess of 130 miles per hour with gusts a lot higher came blasting in off the Atlantic?"

Even months since Irma wreaked havoc on the Keys, there were still sunken boats visible in the shallows on both sides of the road. Various government authorities were removing the derelict and damaged boats from the water by the hundreds and smashing them with earth moving equipment. The remains of what at one time were someone's dreams were then hauled away in dump trucks. Some of the vessels were the dilapidated, permanently anchored homes of the lower paid workers who cleaned the rooms, and served the meals to the tourists and other vessels destroyed were the several hundred thousand dollar toys of the wealthy. Irma did not discriminate.

Sherry continued reading from her phone, "The United States Coast Guard and the Florida Fish and Wildlife Conservation Commission have removed more than 1,600 damaged or displaced vessels from the Keys at a cost of about $16 million dollars."

Mark noted that trailer parks were the hardest hit. The structures are just not built to withstand a hurricane, and were no match for the storm. What the hurricane did not completely destroy the bulldozers were finishing, clearing away the rubble, and making way for a new generation of housing.

Mark said, "You know, you can definitely tell a storm came through, there are signs of destruction, but not the complete devastation I was expecting."

What both Sherry and Mark observed was the resiliency of the inhabitants of the Keys. They didn't dwell on the destruction in the Keys rather they accentuated the resurrection of the islands. As one local told Mark, "This isn't the first hurricane to hit the Keys, and it won't be the last. We Conchs live with the fact that any year between June 1 and November 30, we might need to pick up the pieces and start all over again. It's a way of life, it's our way of life."

The strength of the Keys people was witnessed by a solitary tree growing out of a crack in the concrete on the abandoned old Seven Mile Bridge. Someone decorated the tree with Christmas ornaments and a sign reading, "Keys Strong."

Mark thought, "Like the palm trees that are so plentiful on the islands, the Keys residents bend, but they don't break."

Chapter Nineteen

Mark was happy to see the hurricane didn't scare all of the tourists away from Key West. Tourism being the main source of income in the Keys, visitors are vital to its recovery, both physically and economically. Mark found a parking place without much trouble and noticed the slight decline of people parading up and down Duval Street.

Sherry told Mark, "You go on and do what you have to do and see who you have to see. Don't worry about me, I'll be helping support the local economy."

They agreed to meet at Captain Tony's Saloon on Green Street at a time Mark figured he should be done. Mark left Sherry at the Birkenstock sandal store and walked down Duval.

Mark wasn't sure if JJ worked at Sloppy Joe's or Hogs Breath, so for no good reason he decided to start at Sloppy Joe's.

There were several people sitting around drinking beers and enjoying the ambience of the bar Ernest Hemingway frequented back in the 1930's.

He walked to the bar and ordered a beer. When it was delivered he asked the bartender, "Do you know a bartender working down here named JJ?"

"Yeah, he works at Hogs Breath. Afternoons, I think."

Mark thanked him for the beer and the information. He sat on the bar stool, his butt absorbing the spirit of Hemingway. They were both writers, men of the pen, spinners of tales.

A couple of inebriated dancing girls wearing cowboy

hats and boots, bikini tops and short shorts caught Mark's attention. Probably every other eye in the place were glued to the girls making wild and erotic gyrations near the stage as well. Mark's entertainment was interrupted when the bartender returned and asked, "Why are you looking for JJ?"

Mark figured he must have had second thoughts about volunteering where a stranger could find a fellow server of liquid libations.

"I met him last winter when he worked up at the Wild Whitecap and I heard he was working down here now. I just wanted to say hi," Mark said hopefully convincingly.

"Just wondering," the guy said. Then asked, "Want another?"

Mark declined the beer and turned to watch the dancing girls but they had stopped and were sitting with a couple of guys hoisting brown bottles. Mark finished his beer and walked out to the street, squinting in the sunlight. Even with the decline in tourism in the southern most city, Mark had to wait for the cars, trucks, taxies, bikes, Pedi cabs, trolleys and the Conch Train to pass before crossing Duval to the Hogs Breath Saloon.

At the thatched covered outdoor bar, he asked about JJ and was told he would be in at 3:00. Mark checked his watch, realized he had a couple hours to wait before JJ started his shift and over an hour before he was to meet Sherry so he walked back out on Duval Street to look for the Russian, Yaakov Chaykovsky.

Mark walked into a tee shirt shop and asked the man behind the cash register, "Are you Yaakov Chaykovsky.

The man replied in a distrustful manor, "Why?"

Mark opened his phone to the photograph of Andre Marcel had provided, and asked the man, "Do you know this man?"

The man took a look and answered, "I've seen him, but

I'm not Yaakov."

"How do you know him?"

"He came in and said he was an investor and was looking for businesses to buy."

Mark asked, "What did you say?"

"I told him to fuck off." The man ended the conversation when a customer approached the cash register.

Out on the street Mark thought, "Well, that certainly sounds like the Andre I'm getting to know." He pulled a piece of paper from his shirt pocket and read what Layla had told him: "Duval, near Mallory, west side of the street, Green building, everything $5.00."

"I should have checked the note first," Mark scolded himself. "But then I wouldn't have found out that Andre tried to buy that guy's store."

The shop wasn't hard to find. A young man stood in the doorway waving a sign reading, "Everything $5.00". He was trying to entice people into the store by unenthusiastically saying with a Slavic accent, "Five dollars! Everything is five dollars. Five dollars!", a phrase he repeated a thousand times a day.

Mark stepped into the store crowded with racks and display stands of tee shirts, beach towels, and hats and everywhere were signs announcing that everything was $5.00. He looked around questioning the business model of selling everything for the low price of $5.00, then noticed some of the sweatshirts and tee shirts were imprinted with designs from other cities in Florida and even a few from other states. "Ah, I bet they buy the inventories of bankrupt businesses."

Mark was tempted to take an item up to the cashier and ask for a price check, but he was there on business, not to joke around.

A middle aged balding man with a thick black mustache

and bulging mid-section stood behind the counter on an elevated platform. He was older than any other employee at the store so Mark figured he was probably the owner or manager. Mark saw that the man kept a close watch on both customers and employees, not trusting either. He watched for shoplifters and made sure the people he paid didn't mess around on his time.

Mark approached the counter and said, "I'm looking for Yaakov Chaykovsky. You know him?"

The man eyed Mark with a look of distain and distrust and asked in a thick accent, "Why you wan Yaakov?"

"A friend of mine, Andre Levesque, mentioned his name."

The man looked down at Mark, "I Yaakov. You friend asshole?"

Mark smiled and admitted, "Yeah, he was. But now he is dead and I'm looking into his death."

The Russian said to Mark, "Move."

Mark stepped aside while a customer paid $15.00 for three tee shirts. Mark figured the color of the tees would fade in the first wash, the shirts would shrink in the dryer and in a matter of weeks they would be car washing rags.

The customer left and Yaakov asked, "I no know he dead. He still asshole... dead asshole. You cop?"

Mark replied, "No, Andre's family asked me to look into his death."

"You private dick?" Yaakov asked, revealing he probably read cheap novels or was a fan of late night black and white TV.

"No, just a family friend looking into Andre's life down here in the Keys," Mark said exaggerating his relationship with the Montreal crime family.

Mark asked, "Yaakov, I heard that you and Andre were in business together. What kind of business?"

"Ha! No business. Asshole want buy my store. I tell him

no. He ask again, I kick him out door. That it, no discuss. He asshole... dead asshole."

"Have you seen him since?"

"Ya, he come in few days later, he say he wan be partner."

"Tell him I don wan partner. Tell him to get out of store. That it. No see him no more."

An older gray haired grandma looking lady approached the counter with an armful of souvenir tee shirts in various children's sizes. Mark noticed the top shirt was from Daytona Beach. Mark thanked Yaakov for his time and grabbed a business card from the counter. Yaakov grunted and began counting grandma's tee shirts.

At Captain Tony's Saloon, Mark sat at a table drinking a beer under a photograph of a young Jimmy Buffett and Captain Tony and listening to a John Denver look and sound alike entertainer.

Mark checked out the hundreds of bra's hanging from the ceiling. They ranged in size from AA to DDD, from traditional white to a rainbow of colors, and from plain to see through lace and a few sexy leopard print numbers too. Most were signed by the owner and their friends. Mark thought, "They were probably donated by daring or drunk party girls." Being a Michigan guy one bra caught his eye; it was signed with a felt pen reading "Caseville, Michigan.

He also studied the tree growing from the bar floor and disappearing through the roof and pondered, which came first the tree or the roof?

Mark was listening to *Rocky Mountain High* when Sherry walked in. Her purse hung over her shoulder and not a shopping bag in either hand. Mark stood and greeted her with a kiss on the cheek and asked, "You didn't buy anything?"

She sat, took a drink of his beer and answered, "No, nothing interested me. I have all the clothes and all the sandals and shoes I need. I have bought plenty of tee shirts for Mandy and the baby doesn't need anything so I just looked around."

Mark ordered a beer for Sherry and another for himself. He couldn't believe Sherry was walking from shop to shop along Duval for almost two hours and didn't buy a thing. "You couldn't find anything, not even a stuffed animal for our granddaughter?" Mark asked in amazed disbelief.

Sherry accepted the beer from the waitress, looked at Mark and said, "Na, just kidding ya, I already took the bags to the car."

Mark responded, "Don't do that! I thought maybe you were sick or something."

"So how did you make out?" Sherry asked. "Did you solve the mystery?"

Mark replied, "Later," not wanting to discuss the investigation in a bar where anyone could be listening. "I have one more guy to talk to, but, he's not available until 3:00."

Sherry smiled and said, "Oh good, more time to shop!"

~ ~ ~

The discussion with JJ was uneventful. JJ said he was angry with Andre, not for getting him fired but for accusing him of cheating on his wife.

JJ said the move to Key West was a blessing, he made more money than he did at the Whitecap and his wife found a well-paying position as a comptroller for a company that operated several rental properties. Mark found JJ to be very forthright and believable.

On the way back up US1 to Tavernier and their condo, Mark wondered if he should drop JJ as a suspect in the death of Andre. JJ seemed genuinely sincere in his answers and he didn't fit the typical killer profile.

Mark thought, "He may have pulled the proverbial wool over my eyes, but I'm generally a fairly good judge of character." And a skill developed over the years as an investigative reporter, Mark prided himself on having a pretty accurate bullshit detector, and JJ didn't register.

Mark turned his thoughts to the Russian; Yaakov Chaykovsky. He was a difficult read. Mark didn't know if the Russian was telling the truth or not. He didn't have any reason to suspect Yaakov of lying, yet he really didn't know if he was telling the truth either. On the surface, from what Mark had learned of Andre, he could imagine Andre walking into a successful business and saying he wanted to buy it. And he could also see Andre not taking no for an answer and on a follow up visit saying he would settle being a partner in the business.

Yaakov Chaykovsky was from Russia and had an obvious distrust of customers, employees, authorities or anyone asking questions of him. If what Mark knew of life in the Russian block counties was true, somewhere in Yaakov's past he was probably questioned with much more intensity than by some retired newspaper reporter asking a few questions. My questions, I'm sure were not a challenge to the Russian's resolve, although Yaakov's gruff exterior and short abrupt answers might be his way of covering for a lie. If you don't give much information in a lie then it's easier to remember the lie when you're asked again. Vague answers are another mark of a liar, just watch politicians on the stand being interrogated by a senate subcommittee. They don't lie, they just say "I don't recall, I don't remember, to the best of my knowledge", a lie which is not easily proven.

Mark decided since he couldn't determine if Yaakov was being truthful or lying through his tobacco stained teeth, he would keep him on the suspect list.

"Although, the guy at the first store I stopped in said Andre wanted to buy his store too. Maybe Andre was walking down Duval and asking to buy any shop he walked into. Maybe the Russian wasn't lying."

As Sherry and Mark sat in a parking lot of cars on US1 waiting for the Snake Creek draw bridge to lower, Mark asked, "What's for dinner?"

"I don't know," Sherry answered. "I didn't have time to plan anything because you whisked me off on a Key West adventure. It's your fault if we starve to death."

Mark patted his stomach saying, "I'm sure I won't starve to death for a while."

Sherry, not interested in cooking said, "I know, let's stop by Marker 88. We can get a table on the beach, have a cocktail and some fresh fish straight from the ocean. What do you think?"

As they neared mile marker 88, Mark flipped on his blinker and turned into the parking lot. The hostess led them to one of the umbrella covered tables near the water. They ordered drinks, Mark a beer and Sherry an iced tea and they studied the menu. Sherry said, "The Island Tropical Salad sounds good." She read from the menu, "Mixed greens topped with tropical fruits, walnuts, toasted coconut and a mango citrus dressing. I'm getting that. What strikes your fancy?"

Mark looked over the laminated menu and replied, I should get the Ahi Tuna or the Organic Chicken and avocado club, but I think I'll get the Cheeseburger in Paradise."

Sherry said, "That's not very healthy, ya know."

Mark smiled and added, "And I'm gonna get bacon on it too."

Their drinks were delivered and the first sips were interrupted when Becca Cory, the *Island Times* reporter, stopped by their table to say hello.

Becca hugged Mark as if they were old friends. He hugged her back asking, "Becca, would you like to join us?"

"No thanks, I'm here with a friend, we're sitting at the

bar." Mark looked at the bar where a guy holding a beer in one hand gave an awkward half wave with the other. He looked vaguely familiar, but Mark couldn't quite place the face.

Becca said to Mark," I think you know my date, Deputy Radak." Becca waved him over. When the man arrived Mark made a joke about him being out of uniform and shook hands saying, "It nice to see you again Deputy."

The Deputy said, "Its Brandon, I'm off duty now."

"I didn't know you two were seeing one another," Mark said.

Becca answered, "Yeah, for a few weeks. Actually you fixed us up."

Mark looked at her questioningly.

Becca explained, "I was bugging Brandon for information about the body you found in the bay and one thing led to another and now we're here."

Mark didn't say anything about him being hired to check into Andre's death and he knew Sherry wouldn't say anything either. He didn't want to complicate his relationship with either the reporter or the Deputy. Mark preferred they thought he was just a nosy retired reporter who had questions about the body he found floating in the bay.

Sherry told Becca they had taken a trip to Key West and began telling her of all the cute clothes she bought for their granddaughter, and Mark asked Brandon how the investigation into Andre's murder was progressing.

Becca and Brandon ended up joining them at their table and the conversation centered around the only thing they all had in common... the body in the bay.

Mark found out more from Becca than the Deputy. She could talk openly while Brandon was bound by policy and ethics to restrict his thoughts to commonly known facts of the case. He couldn't, and shouldn't reveal facts about a homicide currently under investigation and Mark respected that.

But through Becca, Mark found out the police had a person of interest they were investigating. Mark wondered who this person of interest was, but she said she didn't know and Brandon wasn't talking. Mark wondered if it was one of the same suspects he uncovered or if it was someone new or maybe someone he overlooked.

Once home, Mark sat down with his notebook to record notes of his conversations of the day. But first he opened to the last page and dutifully wrote down his expenses; the date and miles to and from Key West and the price of the two beers he bought while gathering information from the bartenders. Mark said to himself as he wrote, "If I'm going to be forced to investigate this murder then they're going to pay for all costs incurred. Every single penny."

Chapter Twenty

Mark still had to check out Thomas Minor, the man who claimed, as he was being carted off to jail, that Andre had ruined his life. Layla, Piper and Grant said that they never saw Tommy again.

Tommy was a suspect, but Mark needed more than just his name to find him. Mark called Layla to see if she knew how to reach Tommy Minor. She wasn't able to help; she didn't know where he came from or where he went.

Marcel didn't want anyone at the Wild Whitecap to know that Mark was looking into the death so he couldn't just walk in the resort office and ask for Tommy's contact information. "But I'm sure Marcel can get it for me."

Mark emailed Marcel asking if he would contact the resort and see if they had an address or phone number for a former employee; Thomas Minor.

Within the hour Marcel returned the message with a cell number and an address in Minooka, Illinois. First Mark dialed the phone number but the number was no longer in service. Next he did a White Pages reverse search using the address Marcel provided and found the address belonged to a Mr. and Mrs. Thomas and Linda Minor.

"Probably Tommy's parents." But there was no phone number or email address listed.

Mark did a search on Facebook to see if a Thomas Minor had an account. There were several but none that seemed to be his Tommy Minor, either too old or too young. Mark opened the Google search page and typed in Minor, Thomas. After he filtered out the advertisements and suggested Facebook pages, Mark found a posting for a Thomas Minor in Minooka, Illinois.

Mark said aloud, "Ah, now we're getting somewhere."

Mark clicked on the post and read that Thomas Minor was found guilty of attempted bank robbery in Illinois and was serving an eight to ten-year sentence in Joliet. From the dates provided, Mark determined Tommy was incarcerated at the time Andre was murdered. Mark scratched Tommy off his list of suspects.

Sherry was out to lunch with the condo ladies so Mark had a quiet afternoon to work. He was sitting on the balcony concentrating on his main character murdering someone in Alibates Flint Quarry National Park in Fritch, Texas when there was a knock at the door. Mark put the laptop down and walked to the door. There wasn't anyone there. "Odd," he thought. "I could have sworn I heard a knock." As he pivoted to return to the balcony Mark noticed a package outside his door. "The books!" he said excitedly.

Mark carried the box inside and quickly cut open the sealing tape. He pulled out the packing material and there sat the copies of his book, *Ozark, Lake of Death*. Mark had seen several possible covers for the book that the publisher's art department produced, but this was the first he had actually seen the finished product.

The cover's background was a nautical chart of the Lake of the Ozarks with the title *Ozark, Lake of Death* emblazed across the top in red text dripping drops of blood. Below was printed; *by Mark Daniels*. He flipped the book over and read the back cover;

Follow Will Mellard, a maniacal serial killer, as he stalks the residents and visitors of the Lake of the Ozarks. The murderer wreaks havoc through the popular recreation area as he viciously hangs, shoots, stabs, drowns, poisons and beats people to death. The residents of the cities and towns of the area and those inhabiting the homes and cottages lining the lake are terrorized and held captive in fear. They all want to know, "Who will be next?"

Below, Mark saw himself looking back. Sherry took his author's photograph. He remembered how they argued, or rather discussed, whether he should be smiling, have a stern expression or maybe a thoughtful look. However, Sherry flatly rejected Marks humorous idea of him posing in a tweed jacket with leather elbow patches, a Sherlock Holmes style hat and a smoking Calabash pipe between his lips. The thoughtful photograph won out.

He flipped through the pages, pausing randomly to read passages that he had written well over a year earlier. Some he could recite word for word and others he couldn't remember writing.

To celebrate his first published book, Mark mixed some rum in his iced tea with a squeeze of key lime and took the book out in the sun on the balcony. He looked at the cover again and was pleased with the job the graphic artist did. He looked at his photograph on the back and jokingly thought he would have preferred the Sherlock look better. Mark sipped his drink and re-read the back cover text. "I wish Sherry was here to share in my excitement," Mark said as he read the dedication page; "To Sherry, the love of my life. All the success I have achieved is due to the support of my beautiful wife."

Mark couldn't wait for her to get home, and he texted Sherry that the books had arrived.

That evening, as the sun sank lower over the mangroves in the west, Mark poured Sherry a glass of wine and opened himself a beer in preparation for the condo residence nightly sunset celebration on the second deck commons area. When Mark walked to the deck, he was greeted with cheers and applause. Their friends had planned a party in honor of Mark's book release. There were streamers hung from the ceiling, a cake with a frosting image of an open book, which actually was a Bible and the words, "First communion" frosted over. And a banner hung on the wall that read, "Congratulations Graduate." A black marker crossed out Graduate. The ladies explained it was the only banner at the Dollar Store.

Men shook his hand in congratulations and he was hugged by the ladies. And Terry even presented him with a tee shirt imprinted with the text,

"Careful, or you'll end up in my novel."

They all laughed at it, but some of the celebrants secretly had a real concern of what Mark might write about them.

Mark once wondered what he would do with 20 copies of his book, but by the end of the evening's festivities he had signed and given away all but the three copies he set aside for their daughter, his sister and one for he and Sherry. Anyone else who wanted a copy would have to purchase it online.

Back in their condo, Sherry hugged her husband and said, "They loved your book."

Mark kissed her on the cheek and said, "But they haven't read it yet."

Chapter Twenty-One

Mark rode the high of being a published author for the evening but now it was time to get back to the problem at hand; "Who killed Andre Levesque?"

He would rather work on his next serial killer novel but he was committed to checking into the death of Andre. Mark began by reviewing his notes and found he hadn't completed writing up the incarceration of Tommy Minor. He remembered he was in the process when the box of books was delivered and in his excitement he let everything go. He finished the entry, concluding Tommy couldn't possibly have killed Andre and moved on to other suspects.

"I would really like to know who the police are focusing on," Mark said to himself. "I wonder if Becca could talk a little more openly without the deputy present. He checked the time on his phone and said, "I better wait until at least 8:00 am," forgetting how early he awoke that morning.

Mark turned to a clean page in his notebook and wrote the names of his current suspects.

- Bryce: possibly Andre's jilted lover.
- The guys at the gym who weren't very happy with Andre for messing with high school girls.
- Captain Grant: Onetime friend, now an enemy.
- Layla: Andre's girlfriend until she found him cheating on her and admitted she wanted to shoot him.
- JJ: Mark said to himself after writing the initials, "But not really, I've pretty well eliminated him, at least moved him to a back burner."

- Yaakov Chaykovsky: The infamous Russian. I still can't figure him out. But, for some reason my professional intuition is leaning towards eliminating him.
- Piper: Captain Grant's girlfriend.

Mark thought, "I guess Piper isn't really a suspect, and for that matter Layla and Captain Grant aren't very strong suspects either. Piper didn't have a motive to kill Andre and the other two did but their reasons were several months in the past. But, I want to keep a relationship with them in case I need information from them. They seemed to know Andre the best. Are they suspects?" Mark answered himself, "Probably not."

- He wrote down a new suspect; the person of interest the police were looking into. "I wish I knew who it was."

Mark heard Sherry upstairs and got up to refresh his coffee and make her one-part coffee to three parts French vanilla creamer. She came down with her phone to her ear, already talking to their daughter. Mark handed her the concoction and she nodded a "thank you" without interrupting the conversation. Mark checked the time, not to see when Sherry awoke that morning, but wondering if it was time to call Becca.

"Hi. You've reached the desk of Rebecca Cory. I'm either on another call or I'm out of the office. You know the routine, leave your name, number and a message and I'll get back to you as soon as I can."

Irritated that he had to leave a message and wait for her to return the call, Mark had to remind himself that there were probably many people who called him throughout his career who were frustrated when they got his answering machine. Mark would just have to be patient, not one of his best traits, but one he was working on. "I need to get Becca's cell phone number."

He flipped a few pages of his notebook to the page entitled, "Layla." He wondered how she and Andre met. She said his sexual tastes ran a little left of center, Mark wondered what she meant by that. Mark wondered if they ever lived together or considered it, or if not, why not. She seemed like such a beautiful, classy professional woman, Mark wondered what she was doing with a seemingly low life like Andre. Maybe she could explain to Mark why Andre was so appealing despite his obvious faults.

Mark wondered if Layla could give him any insights as to why Andre was trying to buy into a tee shirt shop in Key West. Maybe Andre was the front man for his family and they were looking to expand their legitimate holdings? Then Mark dismissed the family's involvement, thinking a major crime syndicate from a large north American city would be more apt to try to purchase the Hyatt resort than some tourist trap on Duval Street. Maybe the family had nothing to do with the purchase and it was just Andre stepping out on his own.

"I need to talk with Layla. Hopefully she can provide some answers." Mark called her in hopes of meeting with her. He had to leave a message. "Doesn't anyone answer their phones anymore?" Mark said in frustration. "I wish we still had phones where we could slam down the receiver on the cradle in disgust. If I did it with my cell phone, I would probably break it." Then he said to himself, "Be calm, relax."

Mark grabbed Sherry's coffee cup for a refill and went to the kitchen, by the time he returned he noticed he had received a phone call but with Sherry busy on her phone she didn't answer his. It was Layla and she left a voicemail. Layla said she could meet with him after work at the Whistle Stop.

"That works for me," Mark mumbled to himself.

"What?" Sherry asked.

Mark hadn't noticed she hung up and could hear him

talking to himself.

"Oh, nothing. I have a date tonight with Layla."

Mark was writing a note to himself about the appointment when his phone rang with Becca retuning his call.

"Hi Becca, thanks for getting back to me. I was wondering if you had information about the person of interest the police were looking at in Andre's murder?"

Becca, said, "I really don't know much other than the official statement from the Sheriff's Department says they have a person of interest."

Mark said, "They might have a suspect but they aren't ready to divulge the name yet, but sometimes police departments will put out a statement like that to put pressure on a suspect. You know try to get them to come forward. But then other times the police release a person of interest statement when the public or politicians are clamoring for results and the investigation has hit a dead end. You know trying to cover their butts and buy some time. I wonder which it is in this case?"

"Do you have an educated guess?" Mark asked, hoping she might know something Deputy Radak told her in confidence and she might want to reveal as a thought rather than give a factual statement.

"Well, I heard they interviewed a guy who was Andre's partner in a business involving some sort of real estate deal."

"What kind of deal?" Mark asked.

"I don't know, but it sounds like the deal went south. And the guy lost a bunch of money. But, you didn't hear that from me."

While he was writing notes he asked, "Do you have a name?"

"No, but I heard it's a prominent person in Upper Keys real estate. Sorry I can't help more. But, if you find out anything, let me know, okay?"

"Sure, Becca, I'm just curious," Mark said, feeling a little ashamed of himself for being untruthful.

He thumbed through the pages of his notebook to the suspect page and added; "Upper Keys real estate agent Andre is rumored to have screwed over."

Mark did a web search for real estate agents in Florida's Upper Keys. It provided a whole mess of potential suspects. "I've got to figure out a way to narrow this list down," he thought.

Mark took a calculated guess and eliminated all of the agents and focused on the listings that said they were brokers, guessing that any substantial real estate deal would require a broker's license.

It narrowed the list down considerably, although not enough to know who Andre's partner could be. "Now what to do with the list. How can I determine the person of interest?" Mark asked himself.

Since Becca called it a big deal, Mark reasoned the deal was probably not a residential property. Rather it was most likely a commercial property, like a condominium project, or a resort development.

He made a list of brokers in the Key Largo, Tavernier and Islamorada area who in their websites noted that they specialized in commercial property development. The list was cut down to a more manageable size. Mark added addresses and phone numbers to his list, then turned the page in his notebook to develop a list of questions to ask the brokers.

Mark decided he would just call the brokers and say, "Hello, I am looking into the death of Andre Levesque and I have heard that you were in business with him at one time," and see where the conversation leads.

There are times when luck plays an important role in an investigation. And calling the first real estate broker on his list and finding the man who was Andre's partner was indeed purely dumb lucky.

"Yes, I knew Andre. We looked into partnering on a project a while ago but it didn't amount to anything," said, Lester Gutierrez, owner of Island Dreams Real Estate.

Mark asked, "What type of project?"

"Andre was looking to build a high end condominium project on a piece of Oceanside property he owned on lower Matecumbe. He needed a partner with real estate background, you know someone familiar with codes, zoning and where you may need to apply a little grease, so he and I teamed up. He would put up the property as his share of the agreement and I would do what it took to get the project started; permits, application fees, site preparation, zoning variance, stuff like that."

Mark asked, "Did you check him out at all?"

"Andre had the deed to the property and it showed he owned it free and clear without any lienholders or other liabilities. We were set to go."

"Where is this high end condo?" Mark asked.

The man gave a little laugh and answered, "Still on the drawing board. It never happened."

"Why, what happened?"

"Oh, investors were hard to come by, zoning was a headache, the property had some rare land snails on it and the tree huggers got all upset, you name it and it went wrong."

Mark decided to go for it and asked, "I heard you lost a lot of money on the deal and weren't happy with Andre."

"I was mad at first but it all worked out."

Wanting to keep the man talking Mark asked, "What do you mean it all worked out? You mean when Andre was found dead?"

"Whoa, don't blame that on me. I was mad as hell when it fell apart, but I didn't kill him if that's what you're implying."

"When I found out that Andre didn't really own the property, only held an option on it and I already had a few hundred thousand invested, yeah, I was furious but I got my money back and walked away."

"How did you get your money back?"

"Once at dinner, before the shit hit the fan, Andre had a few drinks and started telling me that he and his family were filthy rich. So I contacted the family and told them that unless I got my money back their little boy was going to spend a few years in a Florida prison for forging a real estate document for fraudulent purposes."

"I submitted my expenses to their lawyer and they sent a check. I was happy. So, see I didn't have any reason to hurt Andre. I'm sorry he is dead, but don't blame the murder on me."

Mark asked for the name of the Levesque family attorney.

"I can't remember, but he had a French accent."

"Is it Marcel Lisette by chance?" Mark offered.

"Yeah, that's the guy."

Mark thanked the man for talking with him and hung up. He then typed an email to Marcel, checking out the man's story.

Marcel, sent a return message almost immediately. "Mark, I commend you on your investigative skills. I am impressed that you discovered Andre's relationship with Mr. Gutierrez so quickly. And to answer your questions, yes Andre was once involved in a business venture with Mr. Gutierrez. And yes, the venture failed to materialize. But acting as the Levesque fiduciary agent I was duty bound to make Mr. Gutierrez whole. I hardly feel that he would want to hurt Andre. Mr. Gutierrez was not financially harmed in the transaction; he came out of the business arrangement unscathed."

Mark opened up his notebook to the suspects page and went down to the entry, "Person of Interest." Mark thought, "The police may call Mr. Gutierrez a person of interest but I don't list him high on the list. Why would he kill Andre months after he received a check for his losses? It wouldn't make any sense."

"So where am I now? I keep eliminating the suspects, as of right now I don't really have a primary suspect. Just the same old ones; Bryce, the gym rats, Layla, Captain Grant, and Piper.

Mark stopped to think about Piper. He couldn't remember her ever saying she had a reason to kill Andre. He thumbed back through his notes. "Nope, everyone else wanted Andre dead at one time or another, but not Piper."

Mark checked the time, remembering his appointment with Layla. "I had better prepare," Mark said opening to a new page in his notebook.

As he drove down US1, Mark figured he would find a table in the Whistle Stop Bar facing the door so he could see Layla when she walked in, but far enough from other customers so they could talk without being overheard.

Much to Mark's surprise, Layla was already there when he walked in 15 minutes early but she wasn't alone. Sitting with her were Piper and Captain Grant. "Damnit," Mark thought, "I really wanted to talk to Layla alone. What's with these guys? Are they afraid to meet with me individually?"

Mark had to quickly switch his approach to the evening's planned questions to a discussion of what he had learned from his visit to Key West and the person of interest the police were checking into; Andre's ill-fated venture into Islamorada real estate.

Layla said she remembered Andre talking about the real estate deal. She said, "Andre bragged about how he was pulling off some big development deal. But in a while he didn't mention it anymore. When I asked about it he just said the deal went south because his partner was incompetent."

Mark said to the assembled group, "I have all but run out of suspects. Do any of you have any other thoughts of who might want to kill Andre, I mean we four are in this together, we all want to find the person who did this. The police don't seem to be investigating with much urgency and by now they have probably determined Mr. Gutierrez is not a valid suspect. I think the police suspect Andre's death is the result of the dealings of his family, you know retribution against a crime family by a competitor. I don't think they consider Andre's murder a Keys problem."

Piper was the first to answer, "I still think it's the Russians. I heard Key West is controlled by the Russian Mafia, they are taking over everything down there." Mark thought it was strange that Piper was the first to speak and that she seemed to fixated on blaming the Russians.

Mark replied, "I heard there is a growing population of Russian immigrants in the lower Keys, but I'm not aware of a Russian crime syndicate. I'll check it out. Anyone else have a suspect?"

Mark looked to Layla, she shrugged her shoulders, Mark turned to Captain Grant. "Anyone come to mind?"

Grant shook his head left and right, "No, nobody. But I heard those Russians are mean bastards, they would slit your throat just for looking at them wrong."

"Russians again," Mark thought.

That evening as Sherry slept and Mark lay awake, he decided he needed to investigate the Russian Mafia taking over Key West. He needed to talk with Bryce, and he also needed to see if he could find the guy from the gym. He wanted to either eliminate or incriminate them.

The next morning Mark sat on the balcony in a long sleeve tee shirt to ward off the morning chill; it was only 65 degrees. He smiled when he thought back home they would be running around in shorts and tee shirts when it was 65. With the computer warming his legs he opened up to email and typed another request to Marcel.

Hello Marcel, I will send an update tomorrow after I interview another person. But I need information about a man who works at the resort named Bryce. I don't have a last name but he has been there for a few years and rents out jet skis. Anything you can find out will be appreciated.

Mark

Mark pushed send, finished his coffee and went to the kitchen for a refill. By the time he sat back down he had a reply from Marcel.

Good Morning Mark, I have sent a request for information on this Bryce fellow you have inquired about. I should have a report within two hours.

I await your update.

Marcel

"I sent the text to Marcel at 6:38 AM and he answers within minutes. Does he ever sleep?"

Staring out over the turquoise blue waters of Florida bay, Mark planned his day. "I'd like to work on the book but I have to get an update off to Marcel. So Will Mellard and his murdering ways will be set aside once again."

After lunch, Mark asked Sherry what she was going to do. "I'm going to the beach, as soon as it warms up. We girls have a book club meeting. What are you doing?"

"I'm going to the gym."

Sherry with a smile said, "Yah right, what are you really doing?"

Mark parked in the Healthy Choice Gym parking lot about the same time he met the weightlifter a few days earlier. He saw the blue Jeep with the black soft top and no doors in the lot and waited for the man to come out. "I hope he doesn't take too long, I feel like a stalker out here."

He checked his phone for texts and emails and found a

reply from Marcel. It contained biographical information on Bryce and results of his bi-annual evaluations from Wild Whitecap management.

Mark sat in the parking lot writing notes about Bryce Johnson and occasionally looked up at the blue jeep. Age 27, from Virginia, lived in the Keys for eight years. Left the resort for a few months when his father was killed in an automobile accident.

Mark looked at the email on his phone and remarked aloud, "No shit." He re-read the dates from Bryce's employment record. "Well, Bryce, I guess I should scratch you off the list. You were home in Clifton Forge, Virginia when Andre was killed and returned shortly before I talked to you."

Mark flipped pages to the suspect list and drew a line through Bryce. "I'm getting tired of striking out," he thought as he tossed his notebook on the passenger seat.

Mark was switching channels on the Sirius radio from news channels, to Margaritaville, to No Shoes radio just wasting time while he waited in the gym parking lot. People walked in, some trim and in great shape, some obviously into bulking up and others who may have just joined or maybe who were not taking the whole gym scene very serious. Mark noticed the common denominator of all who parked and walked into the gym was that they carried some sort of container, probably filled with water or some blended mixture of vegetables, vitamins and minerals or some other health conscious concoction.

Mark switched the stations until he heard Elvis singing *An American Trilogy*, one of his favorite songs, just behind Phil Collins song *In the Air Tonight* and Leonard Cohen's rendition of *Hallelujah*.

As the roll of the timpani drum reached the crescendo, Mark found himself drumming the steering wheel with his index fingers. He was just about to the part when Elvis, in impressive and patriotic zeal sings out with the full orchestra behind him, when the man he was waiting for exit the gym. "Shoot, just when it was getting to the good part."

Mark got out of his car and walked towards the blue Jeep to intercept the man carrying a silver Yeti cup.

"Excuse me," Mark said to the man. "Can I ask you a question?"

The man looked at Mark and said, "Oh, you. I don't have anything more to say about Andre."

Mark reached out his hand saying, "I'm Mark Daniels. I'm looking into the life of Andre Levesque."

The man hesitantly shook the offered hand. Mark thought, "That's a good sign."

Then the man said, "I'm Fred. You a cop?"

"No, I'm just looking into the life of Andre." Mark decided to be honest, "I'm the guy who found Andre's body in the bay, and being a retired reporter my inquisitive mind has questions."

It worked. Fred seemed to relax and asked, "What do you want to know?"

"How long ago did Andre start coming to the gym?"

"I don't know, a couple of years ago."

Mark asked, "What was he doing to get your attention?"

"At first he was pretty sociable. He got along good with the people at the gym. He handed out certificates for half off jet ski rentals at the Whitecap, even helping some of the kids get jobs at the resort."

"What happened to change things?" Mark asked.

"Ya know, we saw him talking to the high school kids, helping them on the machines, spotting them with the free weights, nothing unusual, we all do that. But one of members complained to the club that Andre made his daughter feel uncomfortable. She said he was spotting her and rubbing his hands along her stomach telling her how tight her abs were and shit like that. So we started keeping a closer eye on him. It wasn't just her he was hitting on; he was messing with all the high school girls. Touching 'em, asking them if they wanted to go jet skiing with him. Not just in the gym he would follow them to the parking lot, walking them to their cars and shit."

Mark questioned Fred, "So is that when you took action?"

"Naw, we just kept an eye on him and interrupted him whenever he was with the kids. The management did too. But one time a girl, a cute little thing, probably a freshman, complained to her friend that Andre slid his hand up her sides touching her boobs while he was spotting her. She said it creeped her out. So us guys decided to take action."

"Did you rough him up?" Mark asked.

"No, nothing like that, but we did threaten it. I'm a fireman up in Homestead and the other two guys are cops, so we don't do shit like that. We're not going to jeopardize our jobs for a dirt bag like him. But we told him if we ever caught him hanging around kids again we were going to make sure he was arrested. Then we told him what the inmates would do to him in jail, guys who victimize kids become victims in prison."

"So you guys didn't shove him around or hit him or anything?" Mark asked.

"Hell no, we just talked to him, maybe a bit forcefully, but we just talked to him."

Mark thanked him for his time and they shook hands and parted. The man fired up his blue Wrangler and left. Mark opened his notebook to scratch the gym rats from his list of suspects.

Back at the condo, Mark found Sherry on the beach with the "Between The Covers Ladies" book club discussing their selection, "The *Girl on the Train.*" He put on a swim suit, poured an iced tea, grabbed his towel, notebook and pencil and headed to the sandy beach, the heat of the sun, and the aroma of the salt air.

Not wanting to interrupt the ladies, Mark selected a lounge chair away from the group. He needed a break from Andre and opened his notebook to a fresh page to write about the latest exploits of Will Mellard.

At the Miami train station, Will Mellard rented a car and headed west along the Tamiami Trail. It was the original road between Tampa and Miami. Now days most travelers crossing south Florida used the southern end of I-75 called Alligator Alley. However, the Tamiami trail remains for those who enjoy the slower pace and hope to see gators sunning themselves in the drainage canal alongside the road.

Will drove along the two lane road enjoying what he considered God's creation; the Everglades National Park. He spotted something floating in the drainage ditch up ahead and slowed in anticipation of seeing an alligator warming himself in the sun. He drove with one hand on the steering wheel and the other turning on his cell phone. He wanted to get a photograph of the ancient reptile. He was concentrating on punching buttons on his phone when a black Cadillac raced up on him from behind and started blowing his horn.

Startled, Will looked up to see he had veered left and was taking up both lanes. He quickly corrected and the black Cadillac swung into the left lane to pass. The driver floored his car to emphasize his anger at having to slow for the car taking up both lanes. Will looked left at the car with an apologetic expression but became angry when he saw the man fly by giving him the finger.

Will was so distracted by the Cadillac, he passed the alligator without getting a picture. He sped up to the speed limit and watched the black car disappear in the distance.

"That son of a bitch scared the shit out of me. What a rude bastard!" Will said out loud. "Fuck you! You asshole!"

he yelled shaking his right fist with a raised middle finger.

Will checked the rear view mirror and finding nothing, slowed down again to look for wild inhabitants of the Everglades. Several miles later Will saw a sign for a road side store. "I could pee, and something cold would be good."

As he parked in the gravel parking lot, Will noticed a black Cadillac, just like the one that blew by him. Sitting in the car was the man who pissed off Will so much. The man sat in the air conditioning yelling at someone on the other end of his cell phone. Will's anger and hate for the man began to boil again.

The man exited his car with a slam of the door. He walked towards the roadside store but took a right on a path with a sign in the shape of an arrow reading, "Restrooms". Will followed the man to a row of four functioning blue plastic portable toilets and one with an "Out of Order" sign.

There was a family of tourists waiting for the red occupied signs on the doors to turn to a green unoccupied. Will stood in line patiently waiting his turn. It brought back the memory of going to the Missouri State Fair and his mother calling the toilets plastic palaces.

An older woman wearing a tight fitting Hogs Breath Bar tee shirt and a straw cowboy hat walked out of the larger handicapped porta john. The young boy standing next in line, squirming in obvious urinary distress, started in but the Cadillac driver suddenly stepped in front of the boy and entered.

Will watched and was mad, and nothing good ever comes from pissing off a serial killer.

The door opened in the stinky plastic cubical Will was next in line for but he motioned for the boy to take his turn. Will moved aside to wait outside the handicapped unit.

The family completed the tasks at hand and departed

the area of the little plastic rooms, leaving only an asshole in the handicapped unit and an angry serial killer waiting outside of it.

When the door unlocked changing the sign to unoccupied and the door swung open, Will rushed in taking the man by surprise.

A few minutes later, Will opened the door and exited. He took the "Out of Order" sign off the door of the defective toilet, stuck it on the handicapped unit and walked to the store for a bottle of water and a Snickers.

The next morning several cars with flashing red and blue lights and an ambulance whose attendants didn't seem to be in a hurry filled the parking lot of the road side store. The State Police had cordoned off the portable toilets with yellow crime scene tape and ten to twenty tourists looked on snapping pictures to post on their Facebook pages.

When the medical examiner arrived, she approached an officer and asked, "So, what do we have?"

"Dead guy in the handicapped portable toilet," he responded.

"Who was first on the scene?" she asked.

"I was," he answered,

"Did you attempt resuscitation?" the M.E. asked.

Writing notes in his small notebook he responded, "Huh? What? I didn't hear you."

Not happy she had to repeat herself she slowly asked, emphasizing each word, "Did you give the victim mouth to mouth resuscitation?"

"Hell no!" the officer replied emphatically.

"Why not?" she said, admonishing the cop. "Department policy states the first officer to arrive at the scene of a non-responsive person must make an attempt to resuscitate the victim."

With a gloved hand, the officer opened the door of the

handicapped portable toilet. The medical examiner looked inside the plastic enclosure, to see a man bent over the stool. His head had been shoved down into the disgusting mixture of blue deodorizing liquid, urine, soggy toilet paper and floating turds.

The M.E. uttered, "Oh."

She then looked at the officer and said, "I think we can rule out suicide."

Chapter Twenty-Two

"I'm leaving, are you sure you don't want to go with me?" Mark yelled up the stairs.

Sherry yelled back from the bedroom, "No, I need a shower before I go out. Don't forget the almond covered croissants, get me a couple of them."

Mark drove to the Café Moka, a cute little place with great pastries and an assortment of hot and cold coffees. Sherry discovered it one day on a walk and it became one of their favorites. While Mark waited in line to place his order, he noticed Piper sitting by herself on the outdoor patio. Mark thought, "This is my chance to talk to Piper one on one. Every time I've seen her, Grant and Layla have been there and they do all the talking."

Mark was handed a white bag of pastries and an iced tea to go and went to the outdoor seating area.

Piper was picking at a cinnamon bun and looking at Facebook on her phone when Mark walked up and said, "Hi Piper."

She recognized the voice, she looked up with the expression of a deer in headlights and her lips form the words, "Oh my God."

Mark pulled up a chair to her table and asked, "Mind if I join you?" He was seated before she could answer.

"Ah ... yeah. Hi, Mark. Ah ... What's happening?" Piper stammered.

"I'm really happy I ran into you; I have a couple of questions I'd like to ask you."

Visibly shaken, Piper replied, "Um ... well ... I've got to

get going ... you should call Grant or Layla, they know everything, they can answer your questions."

Mark noticed Piper's foot nervously tapping a rung on her chair.

"No," Mark said, "You and I haven't had an opportunity to talk. You still have most of your cinnamon bun and nearly a full cup of coffee. I think we have time."

Mark observed that Piper acted like a number of criminals he had interviewed during his career as a journalist. He thought, "I think the pretty Piper has something to hide. At least she sure is acting like it."

He proceeded to tell Piper, "I have eliminated just about all the suspects in the death of Andre; Bryce it turns out was in Virginia when Andre died, JJ held no malaise towards Andre and is happy with his new job, I haven't found any reason the Russians would want Andre dead, I eliminated the guys at the gym and the real estate guy who Andre screwed out of a bunch of money. I remember Layla saying she would have shot Andre when she caught him screwing that girl in her kitchen and Grant even said he was tempted one time to hold Andre's head underwater when he fell off the boat, but it struck me that I never heard anything from you. Did Andre ever make you so angry that you wanted to kill him?"

Mark observed her eyes looking towards the gate to the road. Mark thought, "An unconscious sign she wants to escape."

"Piper, did you ever want to get even for something Andre did? Did he ever really piss you off?"

She was biting her lower lip, then answered, "No, I hardly knew him."

"Piper, come on, you knew Andre. Your best friend was dating him."

Piper squirmed in her seat as she spoke. "Um ... yeah, I knew him, but we never talked," she quickly said, correcting herself.

"But, you must have talked to him. Grant said the four of you guys were inseparable."

Piper's left eye was twitching, "But, I only talked to Layla and Grant, Andre and I didn't talk," Piper said knowing she was a terrible liar.

Mark knew that Piper was not being truthful, he pursued his questioning trying to trip her up.

"Piper, Grant told me you four used to go to Key West on his boat and spend a few days. I've seen the boat, it's a fishing boat with a small cabin, it's pretty close quarters for four people. You were practically sleeping on top of each other, sharing a bathroom and shower. A few days of living and partying in those conditions, I would say that you couldn't avoid knowing Andre, and probably intimately."

Squirming in her seat Piper said in a panic, "I have to go. I've got to..." she paused to think of something, "To get my hair cut. I've got an appointment."

"In a calm voice Mark said, "Piper, you're trying to avoid answering my questions. You're acting very guilty."

When she heard the term guilty, Piper's eyes opened wide in fear. She finished her coffee and nervously pleaded, "Please don't ask me any more questions. I don't know anything about Andre, he's dead just let it go."

"Piper, you flinched when I said you couldn't avoid knowing Andre intimately. Were you and Andre involved?"

The tears that began to roll down her cheeks were a dead giveaway that Mark was on to something. He decided to pursue it. "Piper, you and Andre were having an affair, weren't you?"

She was unconsciously tapping a finger on her empty coffee cup. She didn't deny it. Mark knew he was on the right path.

"Hey, I'm not judging, I don't care and I won't tell anyone but you and Andre were having an affair, weren't you?" Mark pressed.

She squirmed uncomfortably in her chair, then she said, "It was only for a few months ... It didn't mean anything ... It was a mistake. Please don't tell Grant and Layla. I'll lose them both and I really love Grant. Please don't tell them," she begged.

Mark knew he had Piper right where he needed her. Emotionally, she was defeated. She was at the point where she had to tell what happened to ease the pain of keeping it a secret. In a clam voice he said, "Tell me what happened."

Chapter Twenty-Three

Piper couldn't resist unleashing the lie that she had been living. "He was charming, he showed attention to me, attention Grant didn't. He made me feel wanted. And we began talking and the next thing I knew we were in bed and he awoke a passion and sexual sensations I had never experienced." Piper spoke freely, the words releasing her from the ties that bound her. Mark could tell it wasn't easy for her to tell the story but once she started she bared her soul in a flood of relief.

Mark took a chance and asked, "How did Andre die?"

Piper lowered her head, staring at the table then said, "I didn't mean it. I didn't mean to kill him."

"Holy shit!" he thought. He expected Piper to know something about how Andre died but he didn't expect her to confess!

Mark stood and stepped next to her, put an arm around her shoulders for reassurance and asked, "Piper, tell me what happened."

It was as if a dam had broken, the dam of the damned. Mark could see Piper was mentally, emotional and physically defeated. She began talking. She was releasing the demons that were devouring her from within. She opened up and told Mark how Andre was killed.

145

Chapter Twenty-Four

In an effort to clear her soul of the nightmare she had been enduring, Piper opened up to Mark about the death of Andre.

"After a month of Andre apologizing, crying and begging her to take him back, Layla agreed to meet with him. He had worn her down."

"Layla is an intelligent woman but when it came to Andre, she had a weakness. She had tossed him to the curb many times for things he said or did but each time she took him back." Piper continued, "But this time she wasn't going to fall for his bullshit."

"She agreed to meet with Andre but she didn't trust him; she didn't want to be alone with him. It was when they were alone that he worked his magic, and before she knew it they were in bed. This time she insisted they meet at a public place, a place where there were plenty of people, a place he couldn't charm her out of her pants. She suggested Dillon's Pub in Tavernier."

"We decided that Grant and I should be at Dillon's to keep an eye on them. Grant was wearing those mirror aviator glasses, a fake mustache and a cowboy hat, and I had on a long blond wig, a baseball cap and big sunglasses. From the parking lot we watched Andre walk into the pub and took a table behind Andre, it was close enough to hear them but with his back to us he didn't notice us."

"Layla walked in and found Andre sitting at a table in the corner under a large screen TV. As she walked to the table, Andre got up, walked to her and welcomed her with a hug and a kiss. I could see Layla stiffen."

"Too much too soon?" Andre asked.

"Let's just talk," Layla replied.

He held out her chair and slid it in behind her.

Andre waved the waitress over and Layla ordered a draft and Andre ordered the same. Until the beers were delivered, the weather was the topic of conversation

Andre took a big gulp of his fresh beer to bolster his nerves and said, "Layla, you know I love you, and I know you love me. Do you think you can find it in your heart to forgive me for my misbehavior? I know I have faults, I promise I'll work on them, I can change."

Piper continued, "Layla looked at him and in a calm measured voice responded, Andre, you hurt me. I forgave you time after time then you turned around pulled the same old crap. How can I ever trust you again?"

"Layla, I promise I'll be faithful, I'm a changed man. I'll be a gentleman and wait on you and take care of all your needs and desires. Layla, I will be the man you always wanted, Layla I love you."

"Grant and I watched Layla look at him with an expression of pity and distrust."

Andre continued to plead, "I'll get down on one knee right here, right now to show you how much you mean to me, how much I want you, how much I need you." Andre started getting off his chair.

Layla's eyes flared in anger as she said between clinched teeth, "Don't you dare. Andre, I swear if you get down on the floor I will walk out. Don't you dare embarrass me."

Andre sat back in his seat and motioned to the waitress for two more beers, then continued begging her to forgive him and allow him back in her life.

Andre reached for Layla's hand, she pulled it away. As he groveled, begged and pleaded, a sudden awareness came over Layla, she looked at the pitiful man in front of her and thought, "I don't love him anymore. I'm over him. There is no love, not even a little bit of like. I'm free of his hold on me, I'm done with him."

Layla finished her beer, looked at Andre and said, "Andre, I think it's best if we part ways. It was fun, but not anymore. It's over, I don't love you anymore. It's time for us to move on with our lives."

The realization that he was not going to get Layla back in his life shattered Andre. He stared at her with wide teary eyes and his mouth agape. He was mad, madder than hell, but he wanted her and knew if he started yelling he would never see her again. He held back his anger and calmly asked, "Layla, please give me one more chance. Can we talk more? Please?"

Andre stopped begging as the beers were delivered. He stood up, his hand digging in his pocket fishing out some money to pay the tab.

He picked up Layla's glass by the rim and handed it to her. Layla didn't see the white powder fall from a crease in Andre's palm into her drink. Andre was so adept at secreting the substance into a drink of an unsuspecting woman that even Grant or I a few tables away didn't notice.

Andre began groveling again, "Please, Layla I love you. Let's keep talking, we can work this out."

The televisions were switched to the Monday Night Football Game featuring Green Bay and Detroit. Fans representing both teams, mostly expatriates from the two northern states, had been drifting in wearing green and gold and white and Honolulu blue jerseys. The rival Lions and Packer fans grew louder with playful ribbing and Andre suggested, "Why don't we get out of here."

Feeling sorry for the man who at one time meant so much to her, she reluctantly agreed and suggested another public place, a small café up US1.

The ex-lovers finished their drinks just about the time the game started and the fans became rowdy. Andre stood up with Layla following his lead. She stood and wavered a bit, Andre grabbed her arm to assist. They walked out of the bar arm in arm.

Grant and I quickly paid our bill and walked out of the bar hoping Andre hadn't noticed the white pickup truck emblazoned with *"Fishin' Fool"* graphics parked around back.

When Andre suggested they go back to his condo, Layla's mind was too cloudy to make a good decision, in the drug induced mellow mood she didn't object. He drove not noticing the white Ford 150 a few car lengths back.

I stared out the windshield telling Grant not to lose them. Did you see Layla staggering? All she had was a couple of beers, she wouldn't stagger from a couple beers, something is wrong. I know something is wrong, I can feel it, something's wrong.

We followed them to Andre's condo. If anyone noticed Andre helping a drunk girl from his car nothing would be said, it was fairly common.

Andre's arm supported Layla around the waist as he pushed the up button on the elevator.

The stainless steel doors slid open and Andre dragged Layla in the enclosure. He punched the number 3 button and the doors began to close. Andre was smiling with his conquest over Layla once again, when a size 10 Sperry stopped the doors from closing. The doors slid back open and Andre was surprised to see a cowboy Captain Grant and a blond me standing at the door.

Grant threw a right fist into Andre's face and I reached in to grab Layla before she slumped to the floor, then I pushed the three button. The elevator rose carrying its inhabitants.

At the third floor I practically dragged Layla to Andre's

condo and Grant dragged Andre.

I lowered Layla to the couch.

"Why the fuck did you punch me?" Andre asked Grant.

"Cause you're an asshole," Grant replied. "And I hate assholes."

Sitting on the edge of the couch next to Layla, I asked Andre. "What did you do to her? You drugged her didn't you? What did you give her?"

Andre looked down at her and answered, "Nothing, she's drunk. That's all, she's just drunk."

Grant threatened Andre, "Listen asshole, if she's hurt in any way I will personally beat you to death." Grant pushed Andre's shoulder pivoting him around. "Gimme your hands."

Andre's hands were tied behind his back with the cord Grant used to keep his sunglasses hanging around his neck and out of the ocean. When he was confident Andre couldn't get out of the condo and told me, "Piper, keep an eye on him, I gotta use the head."

As soon as the bathroom door closed, Andre looked at me and started threatening, "You better get me out of this or I'll tell Grant about you and I."

I was mad and unlike me I got in his face saying between clenched teeth, "You keep your mouth shut about that! It was a mistake."

He said, "Untie me or I'll tell Grant how his pretty little Piper loved to fuck. Hell, you couldn't get enough of me, rubbing your boobs against me and grabbing my crotch whenever he wasn't looking."

"Shut up! He wouldn't believe you anyway."

"Oh yes he will, when I mention that cute little birthmark. Now how would I know about it if I hadn't seen it for myself?"

I was being blackmailed by a sleezeball for an indiscretion from months ago, I repeated "Shut up! Grant will hear," in a hushed tone.

Andre continued to taunt me, "Yeah, it only lasted a couple months, but how many times did you sneak over here to get laid. You loved it, you fuckin nymphomaniac."

I was pissed, my face probably showed my rage and I quietly yelled at him to shut up and pushed him out of anger. The push sent Andre backwards. He twisted around trying to catch his balance but the glass top coffee table was there preventing him from taking a step and he fell. With hands tied behind his back he couldn't break his fall and he landed face first in a shattering of glass.

Grant came running from the bathroom, holding up his shorts. "What the hell was that?" He stopped when he saw Andre lying face down on the table in a pile of broken glass. His hands went to either side of his head in disbelief, shorts falling around his ankles. "What the fuck? Piper, what the fuck?"

I was standing over Andre's body. "I didn't mean it, I pushed him but I didn't mean to hurt him. I just pushed him and he fell."

Grant pulled up his shorts and asked, "Is he okay?"

"I don't know, he hasn't moved. Oh Grant, I didn't kill him, did I?"

Grant stepped close to the table, glass crunching beneath the soles of his deck shoes. He bent to look at Andre's face. Andre's eyes stared blankly, his mouth agape.

"He can't be dead, he just fell," I said.

"I don't know, but he looks dead." Grant grabbed Andre's shoulder turning him on his side. His head flopped to the side. I checked for signs of breathing, nothing, then I saw blood and a piece of glass sticking out of his chest.

"Oh my God, I killed him! I killed him!" I began screaming. "Oh shit, I killed him! Grant what are we going to do? I killed him."

Grant dropped Andre and held me trying to calm me.

"Piper, I've got you. Don't worry, I'll take care of it. I'll fix it. I just need to think."

I went to check on Layla. I stroked Layla's hair and with tears flowing down my cheeks, I said to her, "I'm sorry Layla, but I couldn't let him hurt you again. I didn't mean to kill him."

"Mark, I was trying to convince myself that I was happy Andre was dead because of what he did to Layla, but I was happy my affair with him would not come out, and Mark, please don't say anything."

Grant said, grabbing Andre under the arms and lifting the body from the table, "We gotta move him so we can clean up."

Grant dragged the body, its heels leaving two trails through the shattered glass. I could see Andre's bloodied shirt, the glass sticking out of his chest, the stare of dead eyes and the full realization of what I had done struck me. "I killed him. Oh God, I killed him." With thoughts of Sunday school from my youth I said, "I'm going to hell."

Grant lowered the body to the tile floor. He reached for the glass sticking in Andre's chest and grasped it to pull it out.

"Grant, be careful, you might cut yourself," Piper said.

"Yeah, getting a cut is the least of my worries."

The bloody piece of glass was tossed in a trash can and Grant went to the kitchen to wash blood off his hands.

"Grant what are we going to do, I killed Andre."

Sweeping the large pieces into a pile, Grant said, "I got an idea. Tonight we'll take the body down to the *Fishin Fool* and tomorrow dump it in deep water. Andre will never be seen again."

Grant looked at Layla laying on her back on the couch, her right arm dangling off near the broken coffee table. "How long will she be out?" he asked.

"How would I know? I don't know anything about date rape

drugs."

"Google it."

Grant returned from the bedroom with a bedspread printed with a beach, palm trees and ocean scene, laid it out and rolled Andre's body up in it.

"About four to six hours, the effects should last anywhere from four to six hours."

"Okay, you'll need to stay here with her and later tonight I'll take Andre to the boat. He should fit in the big cooler, but I'll have to fold him to fit in so I need to do it before he stiffens up."

Grant asked, "Oh, do you have any money? I spent all I had at the bar. I need to get a couple of bags of ice."

"What for?"

"It's going to be in the high 80's tomorrow and I gotta ice Andre down or he'll be stinking when we go to toss him over."

"Oh," I said looking around the living room. "I must have left my purse in the truck."

Grant bent and kissed me on the forehead saying, "I love you."

I reached up hugging him around the neck and said, "Grant, I love you so much. Thank you for cleaning up after the mess I made."

"You didn't do it by yourself. We, us three, we are in this together. We all did it. We had a problem and we took care of it."

"Are you alright with her?" Grant said nodding to Layla? "I've got to get a quick nap so I'm alert when I take him to the boat. If I'm not up by 2:00 wake me. Then I'll take him while the cops are busy pulling over the drunks after the bars close."

Chapter Twenty-Five

Mark's cell phone, set on silent, vibrated in his pocket but he didn't want to interrupt Piper as she related how she, Grant and Layla disposed of Andre's body. He figured it was probably Sherry calling, wondering what was taking him so long. He was nearing the conclusion of the investigation; Sherry would have to wait. Mark wanted to hear all Piper had to tell while she was willing to tell it.

~ ~ ~

"Grant knocked on the door, and I checked through the peephole before I'd open it. When he walked into Andre's condo, Layla was sitting up. He said she looked as if she had been hit by a semi-truck. Her eyes were sunk in dark circles, her skin was pale, almost translucent, and her hair was matted. She held a shaking cup of coffee with two hands and looked up at Grant.

"I'm sorry I brought you and Piper into all of this. I should have just gone by myself, told him we were done and that would have been it. Now, we're mixed up in something bad, very bad. I mean we could end up in prison."

Grant went to her side put an arm around her shoulder and told her, "Hey, we were all in this long before tonight. We just to need to stick together and tell the same story and we will be alright."

Layla smiled and thanked Grant.

I got him a beer from Andre's refrigerator. When he took it, Grant said, "I ain't had a beer at 3:30 in the morning in a long time, but I can definitely use it this morning." He said, "You cleaned up."

155

I dragged the broken table out of the room, the glass was cleaned up and I had mopped up the blood.

"Good job, Babe."

Layla asked, "What did you do with, ah... what did you do with him?"

Grant took a big swig of his beer then replied. "Andre is the catch of the day in the big cooler on *Fishin Fool*. Tomorrow we'll take a ride out beyond the reef and dump him. With a couple cement blocks, he'll never be found."

I was drinking one of Andre's beers too and asked, "How do we explain Andre being gone? I mean, someone is bound to notice."

Grant said, "I don't know, ain't figured that out yet."

"We could say that he went back to Canada," I suggested.

Grant responded, "Yeah, but what if his family comes down looking for him? Then what?"

Layla spoke up with an idea, "Andre was trying to work a deal down in Key West, maybe the deal fell through and the Key West people killed him."

I asked, "Do you think that is believable?"

"I think it's pretty good," Grant said. "Didn't he say he was dealing with some Russian guys down there? I heard the Russian mafia is taking over Key West and they're mean son of a bitches. Those guys killing Andre is believable. We'll have to keep thinking about it. But I've got to get some sleep, we have to take a long boat ride tomorrow."

"Hon, don't you have a charter in the morning?" Piper asked.

"Oh shit! Yeah. I'll have to cancel. Can't have some snowbird from Vermont on board with Andre in the cooler."

Chapter Twenty-Six

"**W**ake up Grant," I said shaking him. "You have to cancel your charter. It's blowing like a mother out there anyway. You got a weather alert on your phone a while ago."

"But, we gotta dump our cargo," was Grant's first thought.

Piper continued telling Mark her story, Layla and I were in the kitchen cooking eggs and bacon when Grant appeared from the bedroom. "We have a problem."

I was the first to respond, "No shit, we've got a dead guy in the cooler on the boat. I'd say that's a problem."

"Yeah, but the bigger problem is that Hawks Chanel is kicking up and we can't go out. And they say it may keep up for a few days."

"We're going to need more ice," Piper said.

Layla said as she was trying to flip the eggs over without breaking the yoke, "I was thinking, if Andre was killed by guys down in Key West, why is his car still here in the parking lot?"

"Good thinking," Grant said. "We need to get his car down to Key West. Man if we are going to get away with this we need to think of all of the details."

"Yeah, like why has there been a white pickup truck in the parking lot overnight with the *Fishin Fool* logo plastered all over it?" Layla said. "We need to be careful and smart."

Piper told Mark she was worried I wouldn't be able to keep the secret and told them, "Guys, I'm not good at this. I don't lie good; people see right through me. My mom always knew when I was lying, I couldn't get away with anything. I'm afraid I won't be able to think fast enough if people start asking me questions about Andre. I'll probably just break down crying. I don't handle stress very well."

Layla hugged me and told me, "It's okay, sweetie, we will be with you and Grant and I can answer the questions."

Grant joined in, "We are in this together and we will stick together."

Chapter Twenty-Seven

When Mark finally got back to the condo Sherry asked, "Where have you been? I was ready to start calling hospitals looking for you."

"I ran into Piper and she was in a talkative mood. So I listened and I learned a lot. Your almond croissants are on the counter. I've got to write down some notes before I forget them."

With a rum spiked iced tea at his side, the laptop at the ready and a view of the clear blue waters of Florida Bay, Mark began to type. In outline fashion he recorded how Layla met with Andre, how he drugged her, took her back to his place, how Piper and Grant interrupted Andre, how Piper pushed Andre and he fell on the coffee table, how a piece of glass... Mark's cell phone interrupted his writing.

He looked at the screen to see it was Grant. "That didn't take long. I just left Piper 20 minutes ago."

"Hello," Mark answered.

Grant replied, "We gotta talk!"

"Yes, that would be good. When?"

Grant suggested his apartment, but Mark countered, "How about the Whistle Stop as usual?" Now that Mark knew they killed Andre, he didn't want to meet with them in private. Not that he thought they might decide to eliminate the only other person who knew their secret, but he wasn't going to take a chance either.

Grant said, "No, too many ears there. How about Lorelei's, we can get a table on the beach away from the crowd?"

"That works for me, when?"

Grant replied, "How about an hour."

"Let's make it an hour and a half. I have a few things to take care of," Mark said purposely flexing his muscles for the other alpha male. "Will the girls be there too?"

"Yeah, we will all be there."

"Hey Mark, you didn't tell anyone what Piper said did you?"

"No," Mark answered, then for insurance he added, "But I wrote it all down and emailed a copy to a journalist friend in Detroit."

"Oh," Grant said surprised Mark had taken the precaution, "The friend will keep his mouth shut, won't he?"

"Yes, he won't say a thing. He won't even open it unless he needs too. See you in an hour and a half."

Mark wanted the extra time to finish writing the transcription of his conversation with Piper. He decided the idea of an insurance copy of the information was a good idea and he continued typing. When he was finished, he saved it to Dropbox and emailed a copy to Sherry's address.

Before he left to meet Layla, Piper and Grant Mark filled in Sherry on Piper's confession and told her where she could find a copy of it. She didn't like it but then she was accustomed to her husband's secrecy. She was the person he trusted most on this earth and he had often told her about cases he was investigating and entrusted her with incriminating documents.

"I wish you wouldn't get involved in this stuff. It scares me," Sherry said to Mark as she hugged him, then added. "You be careful! Call me as soon as you get in the car to come home and let me know you're alright."

Mark kissed her on the cheek and said, "I'm always careful. I'll make sure to call."

As he drove to the beach bar, Mark didn't know what to expect. Would they be defiant and claim Piper was delusional and prone to exaggeration? Would they roll over like a puppy dog and beg for him not to turn them in? Would they try to threaten him with death if he informed the Levesque family who killed their son? Would Layla and Grant turn on Piper and say she did it all by herself, claiming they weren't involved.

Mark took the precautions he had learned over his years dealing with some of the worst and most cunning criminals while working at the Free Press. He backed in a parking place in case he had to get out quickly. He arrived extra early so he could select the table and sit with a full view of Lorelei's beach. He wanted to control the situation. He didn't want anyone sneaking up behind him. He wanted the upper hand since he was dealing with amateurs and amateurs are unpredictable.

Mark pulled his cell out of his pocket and opened up the record function. He set it to start recording as soon as he reached in his pocket and hit the start button.

"Iced tea, please," he told the waiter and informed her that three others would be joining him. Mark didn't order a beer or rum drink because he wanted his head clear to ask questions and analyze the answers and also just in case he had to react quickly.

Mark watched a family sitting on the other end of the beach. A frustrated mom was busy trying to quiet a screaming infant in a stroller, a very precocious three-year-old boy ran around the beach throwing sand and generally bothering other diners and a dad who quickly sucked down a beer and ordered another.

Mark's drink was delivered as his phone rang. It was Layla. "We're on the way. Traffic is terrible, I guess there was an accident on the highway, but we'll be there soon. Sorry."

"No problem. I'm here at a table on the beach back by the mangroves."

"Okay, have another beer and we will be there as soon as we can," Layla said.

Mark hung up, reset his phone to record and sipped his tea. "What was that all about? She is coming to confront the guy who can send her to prison and she is cheerful, almost happy."

Mark thought, "I wonder why she was so nice to me? Are they happy the truth is out, are they going to try to charm me, or are they setting me up; lull me into a state of comfort then hit me over the head with an empty whisky bottle? I'll have to be ready for anything."

Chapter Twenty-Eight

Mark saw the three of them before they saw him. He waved and Layla pointed to him. A waiter followed them to the table and took drink orders; three beers and another tea.

Uncomfortable greetings were exchanged, the beautiful weather was discussed, Grant mentioned the fishing was good but tourists' bookings were down then they sat in silence waiting for their drinks. The air at the outdoor beach restaurant was thick with tension. Layla nervously twirled her thumbs, Grant stared at a flats boat at the dock, and Piper rapidly tapped her foot on her chair.

Drinks were delivered and Grant began, "I guess you know everything."

Piper started crying and said, "I'm sorry, I'm so sorry."

Layla patted her arm saying, "It's okay honey. It's better this way. We all knew it was going to fall apart eventually. It's not your fault."

Layla asked Mark, "What are you going to do? Are you going to turn us into the police?"

Mark didn't answer her question but said, "I was hired by the Levesque family to investigate their son's death. I have a responsibility to them, not to the police. Well, I have an ethical responsibility to the police."

Grant responded, "That could be worse. Man, the family will kill us for this. Probably torture us then kill us. We would be better off with the police; hell, the Levesque family is the mafia."

"It was an accident," Layla added.

"Mark, they didn't have anything to do with Andre dying, it was all me," Piper said. "I'm the one to blame, not them. Tell Andre's family I killed him. Don't say anything about Layla and Grant. I did it on my own."

"From what you told me I believe that the death was accidental. What is troubling is the cover up; disposing of the body in the bay, that was intentional and illegal."

"Before we go too much further I have a few questions," Mark said. "If you dumped his body in the ocean how did it end up in the bay? The tide?"

"Naw, we never took it to the ocean. The northeast wind had the ocean really ponding, 12 to 15 footers. We waited a few days and we couldn't get out but Andre was getting ripe so we took him out to the Bay one night, tied cement blocks to his feet and dumped him over by the everglades. The blocks held him in place but the water was so shallow he was floating at the surface. We pulled him up and tied one block to his right foot and the other to his right hand so he would lay horizontal and stay underwater."

Mark said, "It must have worked for a while, at least until his hand and foot rotted off and the body floated free. When I found him, his right foot and hand were missing."

The pungent stench of the rotting corpse and the image of Andre's slimy flesh peeling off his hand crept back into Mark's mind.

Grant continued, "We were hoping the gators would take care of him, but that storm we had a couple of weeks back must have blown him back over this way. I swear I have the worst luck. We shoulda taken a chance and gone out beyond the reef when it was blowing and dumped him where he would never be seen again."

"Well, Grant, that's not your fault," Layla reassured him. "It's Karma biting us in the ass for what we did."

Piper spoke up, "No, what I did."

"No, I should have broken up with Andre after the first

couple things he did, then we wouldn't be in this mess," Layla said.

Grant was next to express his guilt, "No, Layla it wasn't you. I should have turned his ass into the Coast Guard when he first tried to get me into smuggling. If I had, he would be sitting in a jail somewhere, but alive."

Piper claimed her shared of the guilt, "No, If I hadn't pushed him and if he hadn't fallen on the glass table he would still be alive."

Mark listened to the three, the stress had gotten to them, their resolve was gone. They wanted their old lives back, but knew they had crossed from that side a while ago. Layla's life as a respected professional was over, Grant wouldn't be a poor but honest charter captain again. He would be a captain who was a poor felon. And Piper could no longer live a carefree life in paradise. Worrying about being caught, worrying about the mafia, worrying about a prison sentence, worrying about their lives and reputation being destroyed had destroyed them.

"What are you going to do?" Mark asked.

"Well, I guess that is up to you," Layla said to Mark. "What are you going to do?"

"As I said, my obligation is to Andre's parents. They hired me to find out what happened to Andre. And now I know and I need to report back to them."

Layla, with a flirtatious smile asked, "Do you really need to tell them what happened? I mean, what if you told them that you think the Russians did it or maybe you can say he was selling drugs and he screwed over his dealer and they killed him or something like that."

Piper joined the conversation, "Yeah, blame it on someone who deserves to go to prison, not us. We are good people. We don't break the law and we don't do bad stuff. It was an accident. Honestly Mark, we really aren't bad people." Mark listened to their pleas, knowing their lives were in his hands, and he didn't like the responsibility.

Chapter Twenty-Nine

As he turned into the condo parking lot Mark said to himself, "I need to talk to Sherry. She is my sounding board for all things difficult, she's my conscious, my advisor, my confidant. I need Sherry."

Mark mixed them both a drink and they settled down on the couch. With the doors closed against interruption Mark began to tell Sherry all that was said at the meeting at the beach bar.

After a while Sherry asked, "They just talked to you, they didn't try to say that Piper made it all up or something?"

"No. It was if they knew it was over, they were caught, they were defeated. They never denied that Piper killed Andre and Layla and Grant were in on the cover up. They just answered whatever I asked. It was like they were relieved it was out."

"Now here is my predicament," Mark said, "I need to report my finding to Marcel and he will tell the Levesque family, a family who is not above seeking revenge on those who have wronged them. I could be signing a death warrant for Layla, Piper and Grant."

"But if I don't tell them the truth and make up something about the Russians or drug dealers like they suggested, then the family may kill those people."

Sherry added, "And that would make you responsible for the death of innocent people."

"Exactly. See my problem. I don't see any way to report back to Marcel and the family without someone being harmed."

"Including us," Sherry interjected. "If the Levesque's catch you lying to them to cover for Layla, Piper and Grant, then they might come after us."

They were both quiet for a moment letting Sherry's comment sink in. Then she asked, "What about going to the police?"

"The police are an option. And if I tell the police first then Layla, Piper and Grant will be in a jail cell where hopefully the Levesque's couldn't get to them. But then Layla, Piper and Grant would probably be going to prison for a few years."

Sherry kissed Mark on the cheek and said, "Honey I don't know how you can win this one. Let's sleep on it and see if there are any other options in the morning."

They both tossed and turned till the early hours.

Mark arose early and was careful not to awaken Sherry, with all of the crap he got them into she needed sleep. Any of the options they came up with the previous night could result in someone getting hurt. But, he had an idea. He just had to wait till 8 or 8:30 to make a call.

To occupy himself, Mark opened the computer to his novel and re-read the last chapter he had written. He corrected a few grammatical errors and got rid of extra words he tended to throw in as he wrote but he was not in the mood to think up anything new.

The thought of holding the lives of three people in his hands weighed on his mind. Depending on what he decided, three people, people he grew to like, could go to jail or worse. Hopefully his idea would work.

He made the call at 8:14 but had to leave a message. Mark made a notation in his notebook of the day, date, and time. He would have to be patient and wait for a return call.

Sherry arose and found her morning brew waiting for her on the balcony. "Good morning Sweetie," she said before he could greet her with his normal, "Good morning Beautiful."

"Have you had any thoughts?" she asked.

"Maybe. I'm waiting for a call." Then he went back to typing on the laptop. Sherry could see his mind was elsewhere and knew better than to disturb him. She knew he was mentally going through a trying time and he was best left alone.

Mark remained deep in thought furiously typing on the computer for the next hour. Sherry refreshed his coffee and made him a piece of toast with pineapple preserves, but otherwise let him work.

From the air conditioned comfort of the living room, Sherry saw Mark take a call then went back to pounding the keyboard. It was like he would sometimes get when he was working on a story at the Free Press and a thought came to him. He would drop anything else he was working on and go into a zone and write.

Sherry turned down a lunch invitation from the "Between the Covers Ladies" so she would be there if Mark needed her. About 3 hours after he began typing like a mad man and 4 cups of coffee, Mark left the balcony, appeared in the living room and announced, "I gotta pee."

The rest of the day Sherry and Mark spent on the beach, reading and socializing. Mark mixed the ladies a pitcher of Margaritas and later at the condo sunset celebration, or as Debby from a few doors down called it, "Wine Time", Sherry noticed Mark was relaxed.

The following morning Layla called and asked if Mark decided what he was going to do. He informed her that he had, but needed to talk with her, Piper and Grant. They picked a place and time for later that day.

Then Mark made a call to Marcel.

Chapter Thirty

Mark was the last to arrive at the table on Lorelei's beach back by the mangroves. The three must have been anxious, they got there ten minutes before Mark and he was 15 minutes early.

They already had beers in front of them, he ordered an iced tea. "What are you going to do?" Grant asked as soon as the waitress left.

"No matter how I flip this, turn it, or spin it I see only three options."

"One: I tell the family the truth.

Two: I tell the police the truth.

Three: I make up some story and lie to them both."

"In all my career I have never intentionally lied, and I do not intend to start now. So option three is off the table, I will not make up some story about Russians or a drug dealer killing Andre. If I did it might start a war between the so called Russian mafia or a drug cartel and the Montreal crime syndicate and a lot of people would get hurt. I won't have anything to do with that."

"So that leaves options one and two. I think we need to work with the family and the police. I will tell the family what happened and you guys need to go the police and tell them what happened."

"But, the family will kill us!" Grant said.

"No, I don't think so. I explained to the family's solicitor what happened, without providing any names. He promised the family will not seek any retribution towards you."

"Oh yeah, sure they won't," Grant said.

"He said the family knew their son was not a good person, knew he was a psychopath. Andre was an embarrassment to the family. He was always in trouble and they have had paid a lot of money to buy off victims of his assaults and paid a lot in legal fees to keep him out of jail. Don't get me wrong, they are distraught that their son died, but they are also thankful that their offspring can no longer hurt anyone. In fact, through a contact I had when I worked at the Detroit Free Press I found out that Andre was suspected of being a serial rapist in the Montreal area. That's when the family sent him to Florida for things to cool off up north. Mr. Levesque said he would help you guys because he considered you the last of Andre's victims, and he had a moral obligation to help you as he had done with others hurt or wronged by his son."

"You really don't have any choice but to turn yourselves into the police and take your chance with a jury trial. Once the jury finds out what a creep Andre was, maybe they'll go easy on you."

Grant spoke shaking his head, "Oh man, I don't know. What if the jury doesn't see it that way? What if they see us as killers? We could end up in jail for a long time."

Mark agreed, "Yes, that is a possibility."

"The Levesque family has offered to provide you with an attorney who will try to get you the lightest sentence possible."

In anger, Grant said, "I'm not going to prison for that son of a bitch. I'll leave and take my chances in Montana or somewhere they'll never find me."

Piper patted Grant's arm saying, "Calm down, let's think this through."

After a bit of a discussion, Piper and Layla both agreed that they thought turning themselves in and pleading for mercy would be the best avenue. Piper said, "I looked it up and the most we can be sentenced to is five to ten years for involuntary manslaughter, and with good behavior we could be out in less.

"Man, I'll lose my boat if I go to jail," Grant said slowly coming around to the girls thinking.

Mark suggested he set up a meeting with a deputy he trusted and knew to be an honest cop. Tell him what happened and let him and their attorney take it from there.

Two days later, Layla, Piper, Grant and attorney Stacey Gonzales whom the Levesque family had provided, met with Deputy Radak at the Islamorada Sheriff's substation. Their statements were taken and Deputy Radak informed them, "You have the right to remain silent. Anything that you say can and will be used against you in a court of law. You have the right to an attorney. If you cannot afford an attorney, one will be appointed for you free of charge."

They were handcuffed and placed in a Sheriff's patrol car and taken to the Monroe County jail on Stock Island for arraignment.

Ms. Gonzales negotiated a reasonable bail and they were released within hours.

Becca Cory had been briefed ahead of the appointment with the deputy and the *Island Times* had the exclusive story of the death of Andre Levesque.

Ms. Gonzales told Mark, "I have something you may not have heard yet."

"What's that?" Mark asked.

"I obtained a copy of the Medical Examiner's report and one thing I found very interesting is that shards of glass were found in the victim's chest wound."

"That is huge!" Mark said. "It's supporting evidence that the death was caused by a fall into a glass top coffee table."

In an attempt to avoid an expensive trial, the prosecutor and defense attorney met to discuss a plea deal.

In the negotiation Ms. Gonzales wanted no jail time just probation, but the prosecuting attorney was adamant they had to serve time behind bars for the death of Andre.

Their attorney met with Layla, Piper and Grant and told them that the prosecuting attorney offered them a deal in exchange for pleading guilty; three years in jail and two years' probation. "I tried to get it reduced but he wouldn't budge on his offer," Stacey told her clients.

"Before agreeing to anything, I would like to talk with Mark," Layla told the attorney.

Mark was brought in on a conference call and after much discussion, the decision was made to refuse the plea deal and to request a jury trial.

Mark then made a call activating his plan.

The next day *The Island Times* published an exclusive. The article was above the fold with a 24-point headline reading, "BODY IN THE BAY". The two columns on page one and a jump to another half page told of the life of Andre Levesque. The byline on the article read Rebecca Cory but it should have read Rebecca Cory and Mark Daniels.

With Mark's assistance, Becca chronicled the life of Andre, listing the schools he attended and was asked to leave. His juvenile record, although expunged was listed; the fights, the breaking and entering, the shoplifting and the questionable sexual behavior.

Mark's friend from the Free Press, Geoff Henrik, was referenced for the information he provided Becca on the background of the Levesque family and incidents he was able to uncover from Andre's adult years in Montreal, such as suspicion of rape, fraud and physical assaults.

A spokesperson from the Sûreté du Québec, or Quebec Provincial Police, was interviewed for the article. While she was vague in her comments, she did say that Andre Levesque's name had been brought up as a suspect in multiple crimes. He had been questioned on several occasions but no charges were ever filed.

Becca had interviewed Fred, a firefighter in Homestead and he told about Andre's behavior at the gym, how he was spending too much time and too much attention to the high school girls. Becca found a girl who frequented the gym who stated as a 15-year-old she went jet skiing with Andre and awoke to find herself at his condo.

Through a Freedom of Information Act request, *The Island Times* obtained the Monroe County Sheriff's file on Andre. It stated that, after a search of Andre's condominium, the prescription drug Rohypnol was found. Rohypnol is an incapacitating agent or commonly known as a date rape drug.

Becca was able to arrange a telephone interview with Tommy Minor, the incarcerated ex-friend of Andre. Tommy did not hold back in his hatred of Andre. He was quoted in the news article that he held Andre responsible for ruining his life and was happy he was dead.

The article continued with business transactions Andre was involved in. The partnership of Andre and Lester Gutierrez, owner of Island Dreams Real Estate occupied several paragraphs. Mr. Gutierrez, with permission from the Levesque family, openly talked about Andre's deception and fraudulent activities, including how Andre left Mr. Gutierrez with hundreds of thousands of dollars of debt, but the Levesque family had paid off the obligation.

The print copies of *The Island Times* sold out almost immediately and the paper's website was overwhelmed with people reading the online version. The comments section of the online article was swamped with people writing in with support of the three. They were referred to as heroes for removing a dirtbag like Andre from society. One of Layla's friends started a GoFundMe page to help pay for their expenses. Even a Florida congressman commented on the case and the governor's office made a call for leniency, (Of course the governor was running for re-election and his polling numbers were down in the Keys). High school girls who had met Andre at the gym related stories of him groping or leering at them while they worked out and a few women wrote about waking up in his bed and not remembering how they got there.

A hand painted "#Free the Three!" sign was placed on the Old Seven Mile Bridge next to the tree growing out of a crack in the concrete and others were stapled on telephone poles from Key Largo to Key West. Mainland newspapers picked up the story and began to cover the case.

Becca was interviewed on a Miami television station which was picked up by CNN's Anderson Cooper and the story of Layla, Piper and Grant accidently killing an individual as disgusting as Andre went national.

From Becca's article about the man some called poor Andre when he was found dead, he was now called scumball and pervert and other equally descriptive names. Andre had become the most hated man in the Florida Keys.

A group of Key West activists held a march chanting, "Free the Three!" and, "Andre had to die." As they marched down Duval Street, customers from the bars joined the throng of protestors, beers in hand, most didn't know what they were marching for they just loved a parade. It was Key West.

A friend of Piper's organized a "Free the Three" event at Snappers Oceanfront Restaurant & Bar in Key Largo. It might have been the half price beer Snappers offered that brought some of the supporters in but when they got there the excitement and dedication to the project was contagious

They sold tee shirts and painted signs on the foundation of the old Turtle Club that Irma had blown away. Those who attended were divided into groups according to their talents; the artistic painted signs, the left brained created a data base of names from everyone's cell phone contacts,

Becca headed up a group of writers whose job would be to swamp the print and social media with articles and comments. Another group sat around a large table brain storming strategy; a petition signing blitz outside Publix and Winn Dixie grocery stores and the logistics of bus transportation to get people to the sit in at the county courthouse the day of the trial. Some guy named Dave presented an idea his wife Pam came up with. The idea was politely considered then rejected. The group didn't think covering the judge's house with duct tape and not letting her out until a mistrial was declared was the direction they wanted to go. And the bar tenders were busy pouring half price beer.

Mark walked around and saw several muscular men in a group. He figured they must be a security team but then Mark noticed Fred from the gym. Fred told him he and some guys were there to do whatever was needed. Mark thanked them for their support, shook Fred's hand and thanked him for his earlier help.

When Layla, Piper and Grant walked in, the bar erupted in cheers. They were patted on the back and hugged. They were asked to autograph signs and shirts, Grant even signed the bra of an enthusiastic supporter. Layla was pursued by a man but refused to endorse his new restaurant whose specialty would be deep fried fish on a stick. Piper was pursued by an admirer and rejected his marriage proposal. Andre's death had elevated them from near obscurity to rock star status.

Just days before the trial was to start, the call went out on Facebook, Twitter, Snapchat and in *The Island Times* for protesters to gather at the Monroe County Sixteenth Judicial Circuit court in Key West.

The Key West Police department's information officer reported that Fleming Street would be closed and only remote broadcast satellite trucks from mainland and national news agency's would be admitted. The police would cordon off the court and entrance was limited to persons participating in the trial. A conference room at the court was converted into a press room and they said that demonstrators would be permitted only in a location next to the courthouse surrounded by parking barricades.

Social media was burning up with positive support, but others used the topic to promote their own agendas. One person who referred to himself only as "Crabtrap" wrote on Twitter; "We gotta save these people from the geopolitical establishment determined to destroy the working class!" Someone who used the name Ocean Wind wrote; "I saw men in black suits and sun glasses arrive in big black cars. They're hit men here to assassinate the Three. It's a conspiracy!"

There were rumors that Bill Weir from CNN would be back in town to cover the trial. Since his coverage of Hurricane Irma in September, he had become a favorite in the Keys.

The notoriety Layla, Piper and Grant received through Becca's article, the local and national news media and the hundreds of "#Free the Three" signs plastered around the islands was not lost on the prosecuting attorney. He was afraid he wouldn't be able to seat an impartial jury in Monroe County. He considered filing for a change of venue but he was fearful he would be publicly vilified and it would destroy his political aspirations. He made a call to Stacey Gonzales, to see if a plea deal could be reached.

The prosecutor reduced his previous offer of three years in jail and two years' probation to two years behind bars and three years of supervised probation. However now Ms. Gonzales was negotiating with the upper hand and promptly refused the offer then countered with a proposal; no prison and one-year probation in return to pleading guilty to the misdemeanor charge of mutilation of a corpse.

The attorneys bantered and bartered for an hour before reaching an agreement to be taken back to the clients for approval.

~ ~ ~

"Mark!" Layla screamed into the phone. "Mark, we have been offered a plea agreement by the prosecutor."

"Layla, what are the terms?" he asked not wanting to get too excited before knowing exactly the terms of the agreement.

"We plead guilty to misdemeanor mutilation of a corpse in exchange to two years' probation, 500 hours of community service, and $2,500 fines and court fees. And Stacey thinks maybe she can get it down to one-year probation. That's a pretty good deal isn't it?"

"You will avoid any jail time and only have one or two years of probation and community service, yeah that's a pretty good deal," Mark said. "And by pleading to a misdemeanor you won't have a felony record.

An excited Layla continued, "No jail and no police record, isn't that great? Oh, and Piper has to pay a bunch of old parking tickets."

Mark, always the one to question things to make sure he knew the complete story asked, "What about the community service, how long do you have and what type of work do you have to do?"

"The prosecutor said we would be doing the community a service if we removed all of the "#Free the Three" signs. He didn't really give us a time to get them picked up but he said, the quicker the better. So we will be taking a ride the length of the islands collecting signs."

Mark suggested that they put the word out that taking the signs down was part of their plea deal and maybe the people who came to your defense and posted the signs would take them down as well.

A week later there wasn't a "#Free the Three" sign to be

seen across the 128 miles of the Florida Keys.

Mark, Layla, Piper and Grant met at the table on the beach back near the mangroves at Lorelei's. Four bottles of beer were delivered and when the waitress left, without a word, the four raised their bottles, clinked them together in a salute to one another and what they had been through.

Chapter Thirty-One

Mark sat on the balcony with a cup of coffee and the computer on his lap. He opened the computer and found an email from Marcel.

Dear Mark,

This is to notify you that our arrangement has concluded and your employment has been terminated. The Levesque Family has asked me to express their gratitude in your assistance in this manner. A cheque for your expenses and your expertise has been sent in the amount of $25,000 (U.S.). Mark it has been a pleasure.

Respectfully yours,

Marcel

Sherry joined him on the balcony and a cup of one-part coffee and three parts French vanilla creamer sat ready on the table. "Twenty-five thousand dollars!" Sherry shouted when Mark told his wife. "Let's go shopping! Now we can buy that tropical print couch we saw and I know you've been eying a fishing rod down at the Bass Pro Shop."

"Honey, you can go get all the furniture you want, I'm going to sit here and relax," Mark said, remembering his vow before they came to the Keys not to get involved in any crime or anything illegal. Last winter it was chasing modern day pirates and this year it was being hired by a crime family to chase down a murderer.

"I'm going to reacquaint myself with an old friend, my old buddy Will Mellard."

After discovering the body in the bay and holding its slimy decomposing hand in his, and living with the reoccurring stench of putrid decaying flesh coming to the forefront of his mind and weeks of searching for the murderer of Andre, Mark needed a reprieve from reality. He just wanted to relax and drown himself in the fictional murders of his serial killer.

Mark sat on the balcony overlooking the beautiful waters of Florida Bay, the blue cloudless sky and opened the computer and started writing;

The clanging of steel wheels on a steel track was like a lullaby to Will and the gentle swaying of the train car like a rocking cradle.

Will was aboard Amtrak's California Zephyr headed for Grand Teton National Park, in northwest Wyoming.

= = =

Thank you for reading.

Please review this book. Reviews help others find Absolutely Amazing eBooks and inspire us to keep providing these marvelous tales.

If you would like to be put on our email list to receive updates on new releases, contests, and promotions, please go to AbsolutelyAmazingEbooks.com and sign up.

Meet the Author

Wayne "Skip" Kadar taught at the high school level for several years then became a high school principal. After 16 years a principal Skip retired from education. In retirement he worked as a harbor master at a marina on the Great Lakes and researched and wrote eight historically factual books about the Great Lakes region; books about ships that now lie on the bottom of the freshwater seas. He also writes about notorious criminals from the region.

Mr. Kadar writes fictional pieces under the name Justin Maxwell so as not to muddy the waters for readers of his non-fiction Great Lakes regional books.

Now fully retired, Skip spends time with his wife, Karen, at the family cottage outside Manistique, in Michigan's beautiful Upper Peninsula, at their home in Harbor Beach, Michigan on Lake Huron and winters in the fabulous Florida Keys.

ABSOLUTELY AMAZING eBOOKS

AbsolutelyAmazingEbooks.com
or AA-eBooks.com

www.ingramcontent.com/pod-product-compliance
Lightning Source LLC
Chambersburg PA
CBHW071209260626
47162CB00004B/1227